dobi daniels

ISBN paperback, 978-1-958987-04-9

Interior Design by Luxhaven Publishing

Cover Design by The Book Brander Boutique

Editing by JD Book Services

Proofreading by Lisa Lee Proofreading

To JC, Grandma D, and DC, whom I love more than life itself.

Thank you for choosing LOVING THE BILLIONAIRE OWNER DOC. I enjoyed writing the story of Dana Adams and Josh Roman. Their love story idea came almost at the same time as LOVING THE BILLIONAIRE HEIR DOC.

It's so easy to accept the limitations in your life as barriers as to why no one can love you or to believe that love is not worth it. I pray LOVING THE BILLIONAIRE OWNER DOC gives you the hope to believe that love is still possible no matter your past, and healing can occur despite mistakes.

Please continue this journey with me in

LOVING THE BILLIONAIRE ARMY DOC, which is the story about Jasmine Banks, Dana's best friend. You can grab your copy at https://dobidaniels.com.

Would you like to be notified when the next Dobi Daniels book releases? Sign up at https://dobidaniels.com.

Once again, thank you so much for purchasing LOVING THE BILLIONAIRE OWNER DOC and for meeting Dana Adams and Josh Roman. If you enjoyed it, please consider leaving a review at your favorite retailer or recommending it to a friend.

Thanks again for your support!

Dobi Daniels

loving *the*

BILLIONAIRE OWNER DOC

CHAPTER 1

$\mathcal{J}$osh Roman strode down the street, his long legs eating up the distance. He had never been in this part of the Dexington outskirts before.

The rundown houses featured boarded windows, trash littered in street corners, and emaciated rats scurried around. Josh felt like he had been transported to another planet. The thunders that rumbled overhead made for a gloomy outlook, unlike what was expected for spring.

He quickened his pace and wrapped his spring jacket tighter around his body. He was only here because of one place—Wayfare Clinic. He'd heard it operated a similar model to the kind of sports clinic he wanted to open, though its sports section had more or less died off.

But still, it was a good example to learn from, and he could get some concrete advice from its director. And maybe he could even stay back after the discussion to observe how they ran the clinic—the rules and regulations in America would surely be different from those of Spain.

Josh dreamed of establishing soccer clinics all over the country. But right now, it was a pipe dream—it required a huge investment of funds he did not currently have. Yes, he was part-owner of a European soccer team, but the revenue generated was reinvested into bringing the club and its players up to standard. He'd only insisted on donating a small amount to support a soccer clinic in the poorer section of Spain where his club was based, which included maintaining a small soccer facility for the kids, providing two meals per day for each child that attended the clinic, and supplying soccer attire to those who needed it. That was progress, in and of itself, but it wasn't enough.

His head jerked to the left. What was that noise? It had sounded like really old floorboards creaking, the kind that he had heard in his family's century-old cottage home before it was reno-vated. His heart thundered.

Then he saw a set of beady eyes staring back at him from a small gap in the curtained windows of the house across the street. Josh felt a coldness wash over him, and he inhaled sharply. He resisted the temptation to break into a run. He could do this. For the kids and for his dream. He had to. Because he was running out of time.

Josh only had a couple of months before his orthopedic residency was over, and he risked being roped into a fellowship of his father's choosing. His father—a renowned orthopedic surgeon and the Chair of the Surgery Depart-ment at Dexington Medical Center—was very strict and expected Josh to follow in his foot-steps. Josh had thought he would be free from his father's expectations once the residency program was over. But he'd been wrong.

He could already feel the ripples of his father's influence from behind the scenes regarding fellowship options, and Josh had no choice but to take drastic action. If he had his way, he would skip a fellowship altogether. He was willing to go so far as to sell the house his grandmother had given him before she died—as much as he hated the idea—if that was what it took to start the first soccer clinic. He'd designed each clinic to be self-sustaining and planned to bankroll each new one with his salary as a surgeon. Josh was tired of being shackled to his old man and his expectations, and he couldn't wait to leave his clutches.

He missed his grandmother. She'd understood and encouraged his dreams, but she had passed away a year ago. She'd been the only one that could rein in his father a little. Now he was left to deal with his old man on his own.

Josh's face scrunched up. Thoughts of his father always brought bile to his mouth. Sometimes he wondered if he was truly his father's son, but their resemblance bore testament to their relationship. Nothing he ever did was good enough for his father—Josh's very existence seemed a disappointment to him.

But there was one good thing. His parents had never pushed for him to settle down. That was the last thing he needed in his life. He was trying to free himself from his father, not get roped into another bondage. Because that was what marriage was—bondage. His mother had to cater to his father's every whim, and Josh was already exhausted just thinking about having that kind of relationship with someone else. He needed his freedom like he needed air. Besides, he couldn't imagine bringing any girl into his family situation and subjecting her to the same cloud of disapproval that hovered over him. Marriage was definitely out of the picture.

A fly flew close to his face and he swatted it away. Josh sighed. If only his thoughts could be driven away as easily.

He searched ahead, right then left. Where was the clinic? From what he'd been told, it should be right around here. Then he saw the small nondescript sign, just like it had been described to him.

Josh hastened his steps. He would make this work no matter what it took.

It was time to be free.

CHAPTER 2

*D*ana Adams heard the wall clock ticking away behind her. Why was time running so slowly today? She dabbed a handkerchief on her forehead. Even though the weather was cool outside, the clinic was an oven with all the bodies crammed into it. This was the one day they needed the air conditioner on full blast, but it had given up the ghost earlier this week.

She looked around the place. Parents and their children filled the tables set up in every square inch of the large hall. Blues music blasted from a radio in a corner of the room—it seemed like a popular choice from the number of folks tapping their feet in rhythm to the beat.

Dana tucked an errant hair under the hat she wore. She loved coming here and had signed up a few years ago when she started medical school. Good thing Dexington Medical Center had also approved it as a site for their residency program.

The place had been around for a very long time—it had been established as some sort of sports clinic but had since evolved and now provided equal care to children and adults alike. There was still a sports field attached to the building that was used mostly during the summer for outdoor events. It had been one of her mom's favorite places, and Dana felt her presence whenever she came here. She missed seeing her in the corner greeting folks and then giving them their first spoonful of warmth and comfort.

Dana tried to help out here at least twice a month, but it was becoming more and more difficult with her schedule. She wasn't sure when next she could make it. Good thing there were always doctors willing to help—Dana tried to encourage as many as she could to join.

But she couldn't wait to leave today. She had a very important appointment she couldn't afford to miss. She turned her head to look at the clock and sighed. The minute hand had barely moved from the last time she'd checked. She still had three hours before she could leave.

A gravelly voice brought her back to the present. Dana smiled at the grizzly regular standing in front of her as she poured a ladle of hot clam chowder into his bowl, the bright colors of carrot and celery beautifully contrasting the clam, potatoes, and cream. The veteran gave her a toothy grin and shuffled away.

"Going somewhere?" Dana turned and smiled at Verma—a plump lady with short dark hair who she had worked side-by-side with at the clinic for the past few years. Verma was standing next to her behind the serving tables, her hands making quick work of filling the food trays for the walk-ins. Dana had met Verma on her first official day at the clinic, and they had become good friends. "You seem to be looking at the clock a lot today. Are you going on a date?" Verma asked.

Dana couldn't help but chuckle. Typical Verma, always trying to set her up. Verma had made it her life mission to get Dana to go on dates, but Dana wasn't having it. She had no interest in just dating. Marriage was part of the package as far as she was concerned, and no one in their right mind would propose to her if they knew her truth. She had no plans to enlighten anyone about it, so why start something she couldn't finish? "I just have an appointment," she said.

Curiosity lurked in Verma's eyes. "With who?" she whispered as she served yet another regular at the clinic.

Dana ignored her and focused on filling the soup bowl for the veteran waiting in front of her. Clam chowder was today's special and the reason for the filled room. The sooner she attended to those in the queue, the better her chances of making her appointment.

"Dana!" a familiar voice called out.

Dana looked up to see Patricia Weston barreling toward her with a young man in tow, his tailored clothes out of place in the room. Average height with steel grey hair which contrasted with her ageless face and with a frame that carried her bulk well, Patricia moved with an authoritative air that clearly indicated she was the founder and director of the clinic.

She had opened it many decades ago, and it remained one of the busiest clinics in the area.

No one knew much about Patricia's background, but Dana suspected that she'd had some sort of military experience given the efficient iron-clad way she ran the clinic. Patricia had a gruff exterior but was a real mother hen. The clinic regulars loved her.

"Dana." By now, Ms. Weston had come to a stop in front of her.

"Yes, Ms. Weston?"

"We have a lot of people that still need to be attended to and more waiting outside, so I've brought some help. Meet Josh Roman. He'll be joining us to observe how we do things," Ms. Weston said.

Warm light brown eyes with amber flecks stared back at her from a lightly stubbled face. Money was written all over him, from his tousled dark brown hair to his Italian custom boots; from the Rolex watch on his wrist to his diamond studded cuff links. She guessed no one had told him it was dangerous to wear such expensive jewelry to this area. She'd met his type—they didn't last three days at the clinic before never coming back.

And she knew him. Josh Roman, best friend to Blake Dexington, who was engaged to marry Alicia Montgomery, Dana's roommate and friend. Dana had seen him around on the surgical floors at Dexington Medical Center where Alicia and Blake also worked as medical residents. Blake's father also owned Dexington Healthcare, a conglomerate that included the medical center.

But Dana was a fourth-year general surgical resident while Josh was a fifth-year orthopedic surgical resident. They'd never worked the same rotation, so she hadn't really known him until Alicia introduced them. But she'd heard enough about him to know that volunteering was something she'd never expected Josh to do. What was he doing here?

"Hello, Dana."

"Hi, Josh. What a surprise to see you here. I didn't take you for the charitable kind." Where had that come from? Why was she being snarky, unlike herself?

"There is a lot you don't know about me," Josh said. Nice comeback. Well played.

"You know each other?" Ms. Weston asked, looking from Josh to Dana. Dana could see

Verma pretending not to eavesdrop on the conversation.

"Sort of. Josh is more like an acquaintance," Dana said. She had to make it clear. No need to give Verma any ideas.

"Then that's good," Ms. Weston said. "I'm sure you guys will make quick work of attending to everyone. Where do you want him?"

Dana groaned inwardly. Ms. Weston had it all wrong. Josh was the kind that never took things seriously, though she'd never heard anything bad about his patient care. She'd even heard from Alicia how he loved to play pranks. Not the kind of person she needed right now. But she had no choice. He seemed to have impressed Ms. Weston for some reason. "He can stand next to me," Dana said. "Carla had to leave earlier." Carla was one of the other volunteers at the clinic.

"Yes, she told me. Listen, I'll leave the clinic in your capable hands. I have some paperwork I need to complete by tonight. I'll be in my office."

"That's fine. I'll take care of it."

"Thanks." Ms. Weston patted her shoulder and then walked away.

Dana looked at the clock and back at the long queue that snaked out of the hall. Two hours and forty-five minutes until she could leave. And now she had someone to babysit. She exhaled loudly.

"What would you like me to do?" Josh said.

Dana felt sucker punched. It was like his voice had dropped an octave, giving it a rich baritone feel that made her insides tingle. She struggled to keep her face schooled as she turned to him where he stood on her right. "Just use these tongs to serve each person two rolls of bread." Dana held out the kitchen instrument to him. "Make sure you grab a pair of gloves first from the counter behind you." Smooth hands that looked like they had never seen a day's work touched hers as he took the tongs.

Dana's skin responded to his touch and she jerked back her hand. What's going on? This wasn't the first time she'd seen Josh, and he hadn't had this effect on her, though she doubted if they'd ever even exchanged hand-shakes before. She had no time for this. *Focus, Dana,* she told herself. *You still have a clinic to run.*

She turned back to the folks in the queue, and working together, they soon made quick work of the rest of the meal service. Dana looked at the clock. Two hours left. She could still make the appointment on time.

Two other volunteers took over once everyone had been served and began clearing the pots and plates away. Dana dumped her disposable hat and gloves into a nearby bin and grabbed a medical coat from a coat stand before moving to the medical station in the next room. Patients were already seated in the general waiting area near the doorway.

The large room had been divided into different cubicles that were screened off, some of which were used for medical consultation, while others were used by the volunteer nurses to administer treatment as needed. Each cubicle housed a desk with matching chairs for medical consultation, an examination table, and a rolling portable sink with its attached storage system.

As Dana walked toward one of the cubicles, several of the patients called out greetings to her. Dana smiled at each one in return; some of them had known her since she was a kid and were like family to her. She would miss them.

She entered her cubicle of choice and sat behind the desk. She felt eyes on her and looked up to see Josh standing beside her, staring at her with eyes that looked like twin pools of creamy chocolate. His nearness caused her heart rate to increase, and she inhaled deeply to calm herself, only to fill her lungs with his woodsy mint scent. Not good. Why of all days was she having this strange reaction to Josh?

Dana forced herself to break eye contact. "Today, we'll have you observe since you are new here. Grab one of these chairs."

"Works for me," he said, shrugging shoulders that filled out his button-down shirt as he moved one of the metallic folding chairs to a place beside her. Shoulders someone could easily rest on. *Get it together*, she told herself and stole a glance at him. A bemused smile creased Josh's face as if to mock her. It seemed he had caught her staring.

So what if she had admired his frame? That didn't mean he could mock her. Dana straightened her shoulders and glared back at him. The smile faded from his face. Good. Now they could get back to business.

For the next hour and a half, Dana saw patient after patient. Quite a number were sports-related injuries, so Dana gave them referrals to Dexington Medical Center. The sports orthopedic surgeon who the clinic had kept on retainer had moved to another state, and they hadn't found a replacement yet.

As she finished seeing her last patient, Dana noticed that Josh was no longer in the room. Where had he gone? As she ushered the patient out of the cubicle, she saw Josh holding a cherub-faced baby next to a young lady who looked like the baby's mother.

The baby reached out to grab fistfuls of Josh's hair as Josh tickled him. Childish laughter filled the air, cutting Dana's heart in two. It painted such a great picture of love, joy, and family—a picture she could never experience. Dana's heart squeezed in pain. She turned her eyes away, but not before she noticed Josh give her a quick look.

Dana strode back into the cubicle and tidied the area with shaking hands. There was no point in tormenting herself. Romantic love was the one thing she could never have. She sighed and then shook her head to drive the thoughts away.

She looked at her phone. It was time to leave.

Her appointment was waiting.

CHAPTER 3

Josh looked at the petite beauty standing by the cubicle. Dana. It was like he was seeing her today for the first time, though they had met before at Alicia's and Blake's engagement party.

He'd felt a surge of excitement race through him when she had lifted her eyes as Ms. Weston introduced them. Josh had never had a thing for petite women, but Dana was a stunner, with her sun-kissed blonde hair cut into a pixie style and those baby blue eyes that threatened to suck him right into them. But more than that, she exuded a quiet confidence without being abrasive and yet sparked fire when needed. She piqued his interest for sure.

He'd seen her turn quickly and duck back into the cubicle a minute ago, but not before noting her change in demeanor. She had seemed vulnerable and sad, different from the spunky and cheery expression she'd had earlier. What was that all about?

Josh shook his head. This was not the time to be thinking about any girl. He was here for one thing and one thing only—observe and learn as much as he could for his own venture. Any other entanglements were not allowed. He was already trying to break from his father's grip and didn't need anything else holding him back.

A hand touched his arm and he started. He turned to see Ms. Weston holding a large workbag in one hand. Her piercing gaze seemed to drill through his mind and expose his very thoughts. Could she guess that he'd been thinking about Dana? His ears grew warm and he coughed as if to clear his throat. "Ms. Weston."

"Josh, would you be a darling and take Dana home once she's done? I won't be able to drop her off as usual as I need to leave right now for an appointment."

"Sure, Ms. Weston."

"Thank you, dear." Ms. Weston patted his arm and walked off toward the exit.

Josh looked around the medical room. Most of the patients had already left, probably going to their homes or haunts for the night, though a few still lingered. The other volunteers were already packing up to leave.

Josh made his way back to Dana's cubicle and peeked inside. Dana was cleaning up the space and didn't look up when he stepped in. "Ms. Weston asked me to drop you off whenever you are ready," he said.

"Thanks," she said absentmindedly. Then her head swung up as the request registered. "What?"

"She had to leave early."

"Oh!" Her mouth formed a perfect O. Josh's heart quickened. "I'll be ready in a minute," she said as she smiled at him.

Her smile blinded him for a second, and Josh swallowed. What was wrong with him? It was like he was suddenly a teenager standing before his favorite movie star. He had to get out of here before she noticed. He cleared his throat. "I'll wait for you outside." He strode out of the cubicle as fast as his legs could carry him without waiting for her response.

Soon he was in the empty hallway outside the large room. He leaned against a wall and shut his eyes as he took deep breaths to try and slow down his racing heart. This wasn't good. What was wrong with him? It wasn't like he hadn't met her before. Why all these weird reactions?

"I'm ready," he heard her soft, silken voice say. Josh's eyes flipped open to see her standing in front of him in a cute royal-blue A-line dress that fell slightly over her knees. His heart began pounding hard again. He couldn't even catch a break. Was she trying to give him a heart attack?

He noticed she wore no coat and he quirked an eyebrow at her. "Are you sure? You're not wearing a coat," he said.

"Oh, I don't think it's cold enough to need one," she responded.

"If you say so." He pushed off the wall and straightened. He could do this. It was simple enough. All he had to do was get her home safely like Ms. Weston had requested. Piece of cake, right? He led the way to the building's exit and opened the door. "After you."

Dana stepped through, and he saw her stifle a shudder as the cold air hit her. He fought back a smile. He'd been right that she needed a coat. But she straightened her shoulders and forged ahead. Was she trying to prove a point? Otherwise she should have turned back into the building and grabbed one of the jackets he'd seen in the coat closet when touring the volunteers' dedicated area. Well, it was her choice.

They strode side by side in companionable silence through the quiet darkened streets. He'd decided not to bring his car since he hadn't been sure if there would be a parking lot available at the clinic. That had been the right call, though Ms. Weston had shown him a spot he could use if he decided to come again. So for tonight, Josh stayed alert, and his eyes darted back and forth as they moved down the street. This wasn't the safest neighborhood, and it was best not to forget that.

A rat scurried in a trash heap on the left, overturning a metal plate which made a loud clanging sound that pierced the air. Dana shrieked at the sound and grabbed his arm. Her touch sent a zap of electricity through his skin, and he jerked. He glanced at her, but it appeared she hadn't noticed and just kept gripping his arm. He felt a strange desire to protect her, and he let her hand stay on his arm as he hurried her through the streets.

Once they got to a familiar area that bustled with activity, Josh slowed his pace, but Dana still held onto his arm. Not that he minded. "Where should I take you?" he asked.

Dana jerked and looked around as if suddenly aware of where she was. She looked down at her hand on his arm and dropped it quickly.

Josh felt the loss of her touch. What was wrong with him?

"I'll grab a cab from here," Dana said.

Josh only nodded and reached out his hand to flag down a cab. Soon one came to a stop, and Josh opened the back door for her.

"Thanks," Dana said as she slid in. "Thank you for getting me safely here." She gave him a bright smile.

The sound of her voice warmed Josh's insides, and he couldn't help smiling back at her. "Good night," he said as he shut her door for her. She gave him a small wave and then the cab sped off.

Josh watched until the vehicle turned the corner. What had happened tonight? All of a sudden, Dana was intriguing and had some sort of effect on him.

The muscle in his jaw tightened. He had no time for any of this. She could only be a distraction, one he could not afford.

And he couldn't give anyone else that sort of power over him, even a petite angel with blue eyes.

CHAPTER 4

Dana grinned at the stunning woman sitting opposite her in the restaurant's private room, glad she had made the appointment. Linda Wang could have been mistaken for a model with her jet-black hair, exotic features, and long legs. They had just finished dinner and were having dessert. Dana had opted for tiramisu instead of the black espresso Linda sipped.

"So that's what happened," Linda finished saying.

Dana laughed. "That's so funny, Linda. You never cease to amaze me," she said.

Linda was Dana's late mom's best friend and her godmother. She had been there for Dana over the years since her mother passed away—her father had died when she was still a baby.

Linda had served as her legal guardian until Dana had graduated from high school and started college, and she had always treated her like the daughter she'd never had. They'd kept in touch over the years and had a standing date each month at a restaurant of Linda's choosing, because Linda was a foodie. It was the highlight of Dana's month, and she looked forward to it each time. Laughter was never in short supply as long as Linda was involved.

The corners of Linda's lips turned up, and then the smile faded. "I have news," she said.

Dana's hand stilled from grabbing another bite of the tiramisu, and she laid the fork back on the plate. She knew without been told what Linda was referring to. She stayed silent and waited for Linda to continue.

"My private investigator found a lady, Tammy O'Brien, who used to work in the medical records department at the hospital where your mother died. Surprisingly, she remembers your mother's case and is more than happy to meet with you. But she's on vacation in Africa, and my investigator has only been able to exchange emails with her. She will be back soon and has agreed to contact him once she returns."

Dana let out the breath she didn't know she'd been holding. This was the first good lead she'd been able to get in a long time. Her mother had died from traumatic shock at the hospital following a traffic accident caused by a drunk driver when Dana was eight. But her death certificate had also indicated a rare blood disorder as an underlying cause, but the specifics of the disease weren't stated.

Once Dana had graduated from college, she'd tried to find out what type of blood disorder it was. Was it genetic? Did she have to worry that it would happen to her as well? She had done an extensive screening a few years ago to rule out any blood disorders, but what if she had missed it? And now that she was a doctor, Dana wanted to understand the details surrounding her mother's case.

Not that she doubted the cause of death—it was plausible that it had indeed been the accident, and the drunk driver had already served time for it. But she had been unable to find any other hospital records about the details of her mom's case, which was baffling. So Linda had hired a private investigator to see if he could help track down any information about the case. There hadn't been much progress over the years, so this was exciting news.

Unbidden tears sprang up behind Dana's eyelids. "Thanks, Linda," she said.

"Don't worry, my dear." Linda placed her hand over Dana's across the table. "I know it has taken some time, but it's almost over," she said.

Dana nodded and let a small smile crease her face. "Thank you. For everything."

"Oh, please. Your mother was like the sister I never had. I still miss her every day. And she would have loved the fine woman you've grown up to be." Linda patted her hand. "Now on to better news. I have a blind date for you."

Dana groaned. "What? Not you too."

Linda quirked an eyebrow. "So someone has already beat me to it? No matter. It's time. I can't let a beautiful young lady like you go to waste, and you deserve love."

Dana folded her arms across her chest. "I'll get married when you do." Linda was still single and had never married.

Linda laughed. "That I can hold you to."

"Wait! What? You mean …"

"Yes. And Mike is a wonderful man. I can't wait for him to meet you. So the blind date stays."

"Do I have to?"

"Yes. I know you think love is not in the picture for you, but I disagree. And Ian is Mike's distant cousin. I've already told him you'd be there."

"Please, Linda. Is there anything I can do to get out of it?"

"Sorry, dear. The date stays."

Dana bit her lip. No one could change Linda's mind once she'd made it up. She sighed.

"Hey, trust me. It won't be that bad," Linda said.

"But I know nothing about him."

"You can ask him when you meet him tomorrow at the May Crown Hotel."

"Linda! Tomorrow is too soon."

"If I didn't schedule it tomorrow, I'm sure you'd find a way to weasel out of it. Just meet him. It's not like I'm asking you to marry him. And I've already checked your schedule, and you are not on-call tomorrow evening."

Dana's eyes widened. "How did you—"

"I have the spare key to your apartment for emergencies, remember? And this definitely qualifies as an emergency. Good thing you always put up a copy of your schedule on your refrigerator." Linda took a sip of her coffee as if she had not a care in the world.

Dana slumped in her seat. *Note to self: no more printed schedules.* "I don't even know what to say."

"Say nothing. Your mother would have done the same, and you know it."

She hung her head. She'd planned to stay home after work and watch her soap operas. Now she had to figure out a date.

"There is no need to be sad, Dana. You'll be fine tomorrow. Maybe this might help." Linda pulled out a small box of Gubba Dubba Bubble Tape Gum from her tote and pushed it across the table to Dana.

Dana gasped. "Where on earth did you find this?" It was Dana's favorite gum but so hard to find in the grocery stores.

"It's a secret. Consider it a bribe for tomorrow."

Dana laughed. "You are incorrigible! Okay, okay. I'll try and have fun tomorrow."

"That's the spirit! To new beginnings!" Linda raised her cup at Dana.

"To new beginnings," Dana responded, raising her fork.

Whatever that meant.

CHAPTER 5

osh stepped into the large foyer and shrugged off his coat. The house was quiet as usual. Sometimes he wondered if his family even lived here. It seemed more like a monument than an actual home—everything was always in perfect place to the point that the house didn't look lived-in.

"Joshua!" It could only be one of two people; only his parents called him by his full name. Josh turned from the coat closet to see his mother, a slender woman in her fifties, walking toward him with a smile on her face. Celia Roman was a beautiful woman both inside and out and could have had her choice of any man to marry. How had she ended up with his father instead?

"Hello, Mother." She reached him and turned her cheek to him for a kiss. Josh obliged.

"How was your day?" she asked.

"It was okay," he replied. Dark grey eyes searched his face. She must have been satisfied by what she saw because she turned and led the way into the living room.

"Your father wants to see you," she said. Josh's shoulders tensed. What had he done wrong this time? "Are you okay?" His mother gave him a worried look.

"I'm fine," Josh said in a snippy voice. Immediately, he regretted the way he'd responded. It wasn't his mother's fault. He'd always been at loggerheads with his father. He couldn't remember when they'd ever had a decent conversation. But on the other hand, she'd never done anything to make things right between them. She always deferred to his father. Sometimes, he wished she had more of a backbone.

He flashed her a weak smile. "I'm really fine," he said as he touched her arm.

His mother patted his hand on her arm. "Okay. Now go."

Josh left the living room and strode down the hallway to his father's study. He knocked on the heavy oak door. "Come in," he heard his father say.

Josh stepped into the study. With its light-grey colored walls, floor-to-ceiling bookshelves, and a massive black couch, the study gave off a foreboding vibe that suited its owner. His father —a tall man with salt and pepper temples and a strong jaw—reclined on an extra-large black leather swivel chair, his glasses perched on his nose.

The tension in Josh's shoulders increased. "Sit down," his father's voice boomed. A force to be reckoned with in the orthopedic surgery field, his father was a man who was used to being obeyed.

Josh strolled in and sat in one of two wing-backed chairs that boasted deep-buttoned designs that matched the couch. His father got up, walked around to where Josh sat, and lowered his lean frame into the second wing-backed chair. His eyes bored into Josh's.

Josh moved back his chair a little. Definitely too close for comfort.

"Your grandmother's lawyer came to see me

today. She left an instruction that I receive a copy of her will thirty days before your next birthday."

Josh's pulse quickened. He'd assumed all his grandmother's estate had been willed to his father, though he'd been a bit disappointed that she had not left him even a note. Why would Grandma link her will to his birthday?

"Your grandmother left her entire estate to you."

Josh felt blood leave his face. Was this real? "Everything?"

"All of it. Real estate and stocks in various companies, including a significant holding in a sneaker company. The total value of the assets comes to a few billion dollars." Josh couldn't believe his ears. He'd known his grandmother was wealthy but not that rich. "And you'll also be taking her place on the board of Dexington Healthcare."

That was great news. His friend, Blake Dexington, would be happy that Josh's family would remain one of the Dexington family's staunch supporters on the hospital board.

Josh let out an exhale as he tried to catch his

breath. Everything seemed too good to be true. Maybe he was dreaming. And why had grandma skipped his father? He searched his father's face. His father didn't seem surprised or perturbed by the news. Maybe they had discussed it before she died.

This news meant one thing: he had sufficient funds for the sports clinics! Yes! He struggled to hold himself back from throwing his fists into the air, only because his father would think it was an idiotic move. So he pressed his lips tight to keep from smiling.

"But on one condition," his father continued. Wait! What was his father talking about? "You need to get engaged before your birthday, otherwise the right of ownership will revert back to her, and all the money will be given to charity," his father finished.

Josh leaped off his chair. What? Engagement? Grandma, noooo!

"Sit down!" his father boomed. Josh sat back down reluctantly. "She left a note for you. Here." His father extended an envelope with an unbroken wax seal stamp to him. Josh recognized the crest as his grandmother's.

He took the envelope and tore it open. A single sheet fluttered onto his lap, and he opened it.

My darling Josh,

If you are reading this note, that means I've gone. I want you to know that I love you so much. That's why I've decided to will my entire estate to you to help make your dreams come true. But only on one condition, my precious. You have to get engaged. I know you are probably freaking out now—yes Grandma used that word—but if I leave you alone, you will never take the chance. I know you are afraid you will end up cold like your father, but you are different. And marriage is special.

So you have a month to get engaged. Trust me, it's for your own good.

Love you, my precious.

Grandma Elena Roman

Josh scrunched up the note and swallowed hard. How could Grandma do this to him? How could she get his hopes up one minute and dash them the next? There was no way he was getting engaged in thirty days. Yes, he was sick and tired of being under his father's thumb, but this whole engagement thing could turn into a really big mess. His original plan would be slower, but he'd be free.

Engagement? He didn't even have a girl-friend. The only way he saw to make an engage-ment happen in thirty days was to either hide it from the person or let her know upfront. The former was a terrible idea and the latter would bring the gold diggers out of the woodwork. The best thing would be to decline the money and forget he'd ever had a chance at grandma's estate. Yes, he would tell his father just that.

Josh straightened up and turned to his father. He opened his mouth to speak, but his father interrupted him. "I already have a blind date set up for you for tomorrow," his father said.

Would the surprises never end? Blind date? With who? This was definitely not a good idea if his father was the one setting up the date.

"I know you are surprised, but it's someone you might know—Alex Cunningham's daugh-ter, Sophia."

Josh had heard plenty about Alex Cunningham. He had partnered with Chester Harrison, Blake's father's nemesis, a couple of months ago and riled up the board of Dexington Healthcare in an effort to prevent Blake from taking over his father's position on the board. Thank goodness he had failed. Josh couldn't imagine having anything to do with the man.

"His daughter just graduated summa cum laude from NYU Law and already has multiple offers from some of the top New York corporate law firms. We think you should get to know each other more."

"We?"

"Your mother and I have discussed it."

Josh scoffed. It had probably been more like his father telling his mother what he'd planned, and his mother having to listen to it. Victor Roman didn't discuss; he only ordered and expected everyone else to jump up and obey.

"It will be good for you," his father continued. "I'm sure you'll find that you have similar interests."

Yeah, right. As if that was possible. His father's and Alex Cunningham's interests were probably aligned, though Josh couldn't figure out how. Alex Cunningham was known in business circles as a hawk who got whatever he wanted. If his daughter was anything like him, she would try and control Josh. And he was not an object for sale.

"And if you are thinking about not going, keep in mind that Alex Cunningham also has a thirty percent stake in the sneaker company, and could easily make plans to take over or destroy the company if provoked," his father continued. "Your grandma has made me the executor of this will, and I need to make sure you don't destroy what she spent a lifetime building. And I have to make sure you explore all options."

Which translated to mean that he'd better go for the blind date if he knew what was good for him. His father would never let him be until he attended that date. It was definitely not a good idea to decline, since his father was also the chair of his department at work. Josh was almost through with the residency program, and he didn't need anything to mess it up at this point. And what was one date anyway?

"We've set up a reservation at the May Crown Hotel for six p.m. tomorrow," his father said. "She'll have a card identical to this." His father passed him a black card with a gold embossed Cunningham logo on it. "She already has your picture, so she'll flag your attention when you get there. Don't be late. Oh, and don't forget you have to keep the matter of the inheritance a secret for now. I don't need to tell you how important that is."

The muscle in Josh's jaw spasmed as he accepted the card. He would play along and go on this date like his father wanted, but nothing more after that.

He had no plans to become someone else's pawn.

"Earth to Josh." Josh turned his head to see one of his fellow chief residents, Stan Temple, a skinny young man with a prominent potbelly standing next to him. Josh was in the ER because he had received a page from his junior resident about a patient that had arrived with a complicated lower extremity fracture.

Josh was responsible for any trauma-related orthopedic cases that arrived through the ER, since he was the chief resident of the Trauma Orthopedic Surgery service. He had reviewed the case and consulted with his attending who had also agreed that the patient needed surgery immediately. He was now updating his notes about the case at one of the computer terminals at the ER central nursing station.

Stan ran his hand over his potbelly. Josh was sure Stan wasn't aware it was even a tic of his. Stan had told Josh that his potbelly was hereditary. Josh had laughed him off until he'd seen Stan's siblings.

"I've been calling your name for a while," Stan said.

"I'm sorry. I was thinking about a case," Josh said. If Pinocchio was real, Josh's nose would have grown quite long by now. But he wasn't willing to tell Stan that he'd been pondering his inheritance and the blind date. His father's warning about keeping it a secret still echoed in his ears, and Stan would have had a good laugh about the date. Josh still had a reputation to maintain. "What case do you have?"

Josh listened with one ear to Stan's commentary while he updated the patient's case notes, his fingers clicking loudly as they raced over the keyboard. He still had a long day ahead of him filled with a skills lab, a Grand Round Conference, and a full OR schedule that needed to be adjusted yet again to accommodate the patient he'd just seen, and there was no time to waste.

"Josh, I think she's hot." Stan's comment pulled Josh out of his thoughts, and he looked up at him.

"What are you talking about?" Josh said.

Stan gave an exaggerated sigh. "Did you hear anything I said earlier?"

Josh grinned. "Sorry. So who's hot?"

"Dana Adams."

Josh's eyes whipped around the ER so fast that he got a little light-headed. Where was she? And then he saw her speaking to someone who looked like the parent of a six-year old kid that was lying on a gurney. Dana looked cute, standing there with her hands in the pockets of the white medical coat she wore over her green scrubs.

"She's hot and a smart cookie," Stan continued. "All the attendings call her the rising star of the surgery department. But she is a tough nut to crack, and I think you have the hots for her with the way you are staring at her."

Josh's ears felt warm. "I'm not staring."

"It doesn't matter whether you admit it or not. I bet she'll turn you down."

"That's a stupid thing to say."

"I'm serious. I bet you a thousand dollars that she won't agree to be your girlfriend, let's say by the end of this month."

"Are you kidding?"

"That's how impossible I think it's going to be."

"Forget it."

"I'm serious, okay? One thousand dollars. It's a deal," Stan called behind him as he walked away.

Josh shook his head. There was no way he was going to involve himself in such a stupid bet. That was the kind of thing he'd seen in college, and he'd hated it. He looked at where he had seen Dana. She was gone. Just as well; he didn't need any distractions.

Even if by some unimaginable reason he became interested in dating her, it would be with no strings attached. And that wasn't even going to happen because he didn't want a relationship. And he already had his hands full with this blind date that he wanted no part of.

Josh sighed and turned back to the computer. The patient's notes would not update themselves. It was time to focus and take care of his patients.

The blind date and thoughts of Dana could wait.

CHAPTER 6

Dana looked around the lobby of the May Crown Hotel. Men and women in business suits lounged on single high-backed seats scattered around the center of the luxuriant lobby, while couples in what appeared to be deep conversation occupied the seats lined along the floor-to-ceiling glass walls.

Dana grimaced. She'd heard the hotel was a favorite for dates, but she'd thought it was a joke. Why on earth would Linda choose this hotel of all places? It was like having a billboard on her forehead that said "date me." Hopefully, she wouldn't meet anyone here that knew her from the hospital.

Dana tugged at the yellow rose on her

blouse. Linda had told her that Ian would be holding a yellow rose as well. It was a little bit old-fashioned, but hey that was Linda—she could be unexpected when she wanted to be.

Dana took a deep inhale. She could power through this. She had promised Linda she'd try, and she kept her promises. And it wasn't like she was going to marry the guy. That much she had made clear to Linda.

Dana tugged the end of her skirt down as she scanned the area for her date. It had been a long time since she'd worn one, courtesy of the surgery residency program. Not that she had anything against skirts; in fact, she used to wear them a lot in college. But her busy surgical schedule had left no room for them in her life—ease, safety, and comfort had become the priority. However, Linda had insisted that the skirt and blouse would look divine on her, so Dana had agreed to wear them. She couldn't wait to be done with the date and out of the attire.

Dana sensed eyes on her. She looked to the left to see a lean young man in a black suit standing next to one of the tables along the glass wall, waving a yellow rose at her. That must be

Ian. Not bad looking. But experience had taught her that the inner package was more important.

She pasted a smile on her face as she approached the table where Ian stood. There was a blonde mannequin seated at the table right next to theirs with someone whose face she couldn't see, but Dana paid them no mind.

"Hi," she said once she reached the table.

"Hello," he responded in a cute British accent. But it sounded a little … fake? She could be wrong. It wasn't like she'd lived in England.

"I'm Dana." She stretched out her hand for a handshake.

"I'm Ian. Nice to meet you." He shook her hand firmly. Not bad. She liked a man with a firm, yet not overpowering, grip. She slid into the open seat with her back to the other couple sitting next to them.

A waiter in a black uniform with a white apron appeared out of thin air as if cued. "What would you like to drink, ma'am?" he asked.

"A glass of water is fine." At Ian's raised eyebrow, "I still have some work to take care of tonight," she said.

"Would you like to order now?" the waiter asked.

"Maybe in about fifteen minutes?" That would give her enough time to know if she needed to make her escape.

"Same here," Ian said to the waiter. The waiter nodded and left.

"Linda tells me you are a doctor," Ian said. "What are you specialized in?"

"Surgery." Dana saw him crinkle his nose. What was that all about? The surgery residency was hard to get into, and she had gotten into one of the top programs in the country without any connections. Maybe she was reading too much into it. She would give Ian another chance. "What about you? What do you do?"

"I'm an investment banker." He leaned back in his seat.

"Interesting. That means you must spend a lot of time in New York."

"I actually live there. I just came into town because of this date. Linda talked so much about you that I thought why not. It also got Mike off my back." He laughed. "It's not a big deal." He looked down and examined his fingers.

So he hadn't been keen on this date. Then why had he come? And why was he playing with his fingers? Who does that on a date? Was he bored? No, it was more likely that he was full of himself.

And as the conversation continued between them, Dana confirmed she was right. All Ian talked about was how much money he was making, this or that stock trade, the cars he owned, and his family connections. Didn't he realize he was talking to a doctor, a surgeon who had the potential to make more in a few years than he could ever imagine? Maybe the spiel worked on other girls, but he should have remembered who was sitting opposite him.

Mike might be a great guy, but Ian didn't seem to be cut from the same cloth. Dana couldn't wait for the date to be over. She would have had a better time watching one of her soap operas. But out of respect for Linda, she would try and suffer through the rest of it until the date was over. No second dates in this case for sure.

She leaned back and settled in. It was going to be a long evening. Maybe the guy would realize the date was a dud and opt to leave first.

Josh couldn't believe his ears. It was like listening to the sound of a train, rumbling on and on without stopping. He hadn't been able to get a word in edgewise with his blind date, so he'd given up and just fiddled with his napkin instead.

It was definitely true that beauty wasn't everything. Sophia was tall, with a face and body that his teammates on his college soccer team would have died for. But the minute she had opened her mouth, all she could talk about was herself, where she loved to shop, and all the famous people she had met.

At that moment, Josh felt sorry for all the folks in her life that must have been forced to endure her chatter. Ladies loved to talk, but this was way over-the-top. And did she really think he would be interested in her right pinky fingernail having the precise shade of fuchsia nail polish color that had been shown on a popular TV fashion show?

It was time to make his getaway. This date wasn't working, and he was not willing to endure it much longer. At this point, he didn't even care anymore about what Alex Cunningham would do. He'd figure that out later if it came to it.

But he couldn't simply tell Sophia he had to leave. He needed a good excuse, one that would make it hard for their parents to schedule another date for them. He looked around the lobby, his eyes searching for ideas while his date droned on until his gaze fell on the back of a familiar-looking blonde.

His breath hitched, and he leaned forward. Could it really be her sitting at the next table? She turned slightly, and he caught a glimpse of her face. It was really Dana!

But what was she doing here? He didn't peg her as the type to go on blind dates. He tried to listen to their conversation while maintaining a facade of indifference, and his lips turned up into a smile. *Dana must want to get rid of her date as soon as possible.*

Any friend of Alicia's would not stand a guy who was only interested in talking about his job, cars, and connections. Josh liked his cars too, but there was no way he would talk about that on a date unless the other party brought it up. Didn't the guy know conversations were give-and-take?

His mind began to whirl with ideas, and one caught his attention. Since it seemed she wanted to leave and he was ready to ditch his date, maybe it would work. But would Dana go with it? What if it backfired or she got embarrassed? Well, he would beg for forgiveness no matter what it took. It would be way better than continuing to listen to this chatterbox. He had to take a chance or lose the opportunity.

Josh turned to Sophia. "I'm sorry. This was a mistake. I have to go." Sophia stopped talking, confusion written all over her face. He signaled the attention of a waiter, pulled out his wallet and dropped some hundred-dollar notes on the menu. "It was nice meeting you, Sophia." He didn't wait for a response, but got up and walked over to Dana's table.

Dana's eyes widened on seeing him, but he ignored it and pulled her to her feet. "Let's go."

"Hey! What are you doing?" her date sputtered. Ah, an investment banker. He had the look down with his three-piece suit, pocket handkerchief, and slicked-down hair. Josh knew his type.

"Now that's the question I should ask you." He turned to Dana. "Babe, you didn't tell him?" By now, Dana was staring at him. He pulled her into a side hug and whispered into her ear, "Go with this, okay?"

He turned back to her date. "Hi, I'm Josh. Dana is my girlfriend. Who are you?"

CHAPTER 8

Dana couldn't believe what was happening. One minute she was on a blind date, and now she was someone's girlfriend? She'd been shocked to feel a zap of electricity run through her as someone grabbed her hand. Though at first she was ready to knock it off, she'd been surprised to see Josh pull her to her feet and then into a hug while he whispered something into her ear.

The hug had been unexpected, but it had warmed her insides, and all she'd thought of at that moment was the feeling of his arms around her and the tingling of her skin where his touched hers. His woodsy mint scent had fanned her face as he'd whispered into her ear and she'd wished she could inhale in more. But he'd soon turned her back to her date. "Hi, I'm Josh. Dana is my girlfriend. Who are you?" he'd said.

Wait! What was Josh talking about? Ian blanched and jumped to his feet.

Dana cringed. All this was happening too fast. As much as she'd wanted the date to end, this was not the way to do it. She tried to pull away, but Josh's arm around her waist held fast. She glanced at his face, only to see his irresistible eyes pleading with her to go along with it, contrasting with the set smile on his face.

"Your girlfriend?" a shrill voice shrieked from behind her. Dana resisted the urge to shut her ears and turned to see who was speaking. It was the blonde mannequin from the next table. She appeared to know Josh. Wait! So he was the person whose face she hadn't seen.

She saw Josh wince. No wonder he couldn't wait to get away from her as fast as possible. One could only tolerate that voice for so long. "My father will hear about this!" Then the pretty blonde stormed off with a huff, her high heels clicking loudly on the floor and drawing attention from the other folks in the lobby.

"Time to go, babe," Josh said. And the next thing Dana knew, Josh was leading her away from the table to the hotel exit. She barely managed to grab her handbag in time. Maybe she was relieved at being done with the date, because Dana allowed Josh to keep his pressure on her back, his touch distracting her until they stepped through the large revolving door into the hotel's covered driveway. Only then did he drop his hand. Dana felt the loss immediately, but then came to her senses at the same time.

She turned to Josh. "What was that all about?"

A bemused smile flickered across his face. "I believe I did both of us a favor."

"A favor?"

"Weren't you dying to leave that date? I could totally tell from your body posture. And don't tell me you were enjoying all that talk about cars and all the people he knew."

"But it was none of your business. That date was set up by someone dear to me. I was ready to endure it to the end."

"See what I mean? You hated the date. And I'm telling you, Dana, that guy would not have ended it with just one date. He would have called you up on a second date just to stroke his ego. And that British accent was definitely fake." Dana couldn't help but chuckle. Josh had come to the same conclusion. "See, I was right."

Dana shook her head. Alicia had told her that Josh liked to play pranks, but she hadn't thought he would play one on her. Good thing she'd only benefited from it and not been on the receiving end. As bad as she felt about leaving Ian that way, she was relieved she could go home, curl up on the couch like she'd originally planned, and watch one of her soap operas.

A familiar jazz tune pierced the air. Dana opened her bag to pull out her phone, but the tune had stopped playing. "Hello?" she heard Josh say.

So it was his ringtone as well. Interesting. Who would have thought? And come to think of it, her phone was on vibrate.

Well, it was time to be on her way. She adjusted the strap of her bag over her shoulder and craned her neck to see if there were any cabs in the cab stand.

"You want to meet my girlfriend?" she heard him say.

Dana froze. Girlfriend? Whoever was on the line couldn't possibly be talking about her.

Josh touched her arm. "Dana, I'm sorry." His eyes were serious as he looked into hers.

Dana's pulse picked up its pace. Conversations that started this way were never good. "What is it?"

Josh ran a hand through his hair. "My father wants to meet you."

Dana felt the blood drain from her face.

CHAPTER 9

"This is a bad idea." Dana said as the cab headed toward Josh's home. Josh hadn't brought his car to the date, so they'd taken a cab instead.

He agreed with Dana. What had started out as a little lie to get out of a small situation had now spiraled out of control. How had his father known about her so quickly? Had he put someone on him to observe his date? No, that wasn't possible. No matter how much his father tried to have a say in his life, this was one line he'd never cross. Most likely, Sophia had complained to her dad who had then called his.

His stomach recoiled just thinking about getting Dana involved with his family. That hadn't been his plan, and now he had this mess he needed to clear up. If his father found out that it was all a lie, he wasn't sure what would happen to Dana, since she also worked under his father.

If Josh refused to bring her home, it wouldn't be too hard for his father to find out her identity. There weren't many with the name in Dexington, and Sophia could ID her. Dana could then run the risk of facing his father alone, which could be disastrous for her. It was better for them to meet him together.

Josh sighed. It was all his fault they were in this mess, and he couldn't allow any repercussions on her career. He'd managed to convince Dana to go along with the fake relationship for now. They could then inform his father later that they had broken up, which wouldn't be unusual.

"What do you think he's going to say?" Dana asked and bit her lip. She needed to stop doing that. Dana probably had no idea that it drew attention to her inviting lips. He brushed the thought away. He couldn't afford to think about kissing her; this situation they were in deserved his complete focus. And they didn't have that kind of relationship.

"I have no idea," he responded and turned his attention back to the road ahead. "But I think it's going to be okay."

Dana let out a long sigh. "I've never spoken to your father before, and I didn't think it would be like this," she said, the pitch in her voice a little higher than normal.

He stretched out his right hand and covered her clasped hands. "It's going to be okay," he said, forcing some confidence into his voice. "Just let me do the talking." He felt her relax her hands a little. Much better.

Josh felt a strong urge to protect her. He had gotten her into this, and he would make sure there were no other complications.

They soon reached his parents' gated home. Josh pressed the fob he had pulled from his pocket, and the gates swung open. He directed the cab to go all the way to the top of the driveway, and they stepped out once it came to a stop. He waited to make sure the cab had exited the gates before he opened the front door and led Dana into the foyer of his home.

His mother didn't come to the door, which

meant she was probably not at home. Good. Meeting both parents this way might be overwhelming.

He led Dana through the cavernous living room to his father's study, where he was sure to be. Josh hesitated for a moment and then knocked on the door.

It was time to face the music.

CHAPTER 10

Dana was still in shock from how large Josh's home was when Josh knocked on the study door and ushered her in. She'd had an idea that his family was wealthy, but she didn't think they were *that* rich. Which meant that Josh's parents might not approve of her, given she was not from their social circle. Not that she was really planning to date him or anything.

Prof. Roman stood by a large window, wearing a grey V-necked sweater over a white shirt with tan slacks. He turned when they entered, and Dana saw his eyes widen in recognition for a moment. An unknown emotion crossed his face before he schooled his features.

"Dr. Dana Adams, right?" his father asked, his eyes boring into hers.

Dana hid her gasp. How did he know who she was? She'd never met him one-on-one before, though she had seen him from afar during the hospital's surgical grand rounds. He was an accomplished surgeon, one of the few people that Dana aspired to be like. Definitely not someone she'd hoped to meet in his own home! She couldn't say a word. It was like she lost her ability to speak.

Josh reached for Dana's hand and held it in his; the touch calmed her. His hand was soft, warm, and comforting, and hers fit rather nicely in his like it belonged there. "Father, this is my girlfriend, Dana," he said.

"Since when?"

"For a while now." Wait! They hadn't really talked about this.

His father stepped away from the window and walked over to his mahogany desk. "How come I'm just hearing about this?"

"It wasn't relevant for you to know before, and you didn't give me a chance yesterday to tell you." Yesterday? What was Josh talking about?

"Is this serious?"

"As serious as can be." His father lifted an eyebrow. "Father, get used to it. I intend to marry her."

Dana stiffened and her heart raced. Where did that come from? This wasn't what they had agreed on! It was only supposed to be dating. Nothing more.

His father's eyes narrowed. "I'd like to speak to you alone."

"No can do," Josh continued. "You either speak to us together or not at all."

Dana's chest tightened, and she drew in a sharp inhale. This conversation was going in a direction she hadn't bargained for. She needed some fresh air.

She turned to Josh. "I need to use the bathroom," her voice came out in a whisper. She'd noted the bathroom's location on their way in. She slipped her hand from his and turned to his father. "It was nice meeting you, Professor Roman."

Dana didn't wait for a response and left the study as fast as her legs could carry her.

CHAPTER 11

*H*e hadn't meant to say that. What had gotten into him? He was supposed to be resolving the situation, not making it more complicated. Marry? That wasn't even on his agenda. It would have been better to just say they were as good as engaged.

Wait! That would work. But he already felt terrible lying to his father and this would make it worse. But there was no way he could suddenly end the relationship now, not with what he had just declared to his father. He would have to ask Dana if she could stay engaged to him for a few weeks, and then they would break it off. If it was shorter than that, his father would be suspicious about the relationship, and it would blow up in their faces.

And it came with an unexpected benefit he hadn't thought of—he would be able to get the inheritance as well. But there was no way he could tell her about it, though he wished to. His father had insisted that the inheritance be a secret, and Josh agreed with him. Even though he doubted any close friend of Alicia's would take advantage of him, he could not afford any further entanglements once he got free of his father. It was better not to risk it.

"I'm not happy about this so-called relationship," his father said.

Josh bristled. Even though this was a fake relationship, Dana was a great girl from what he had seen so far. She didn't deserve what his father was implying. "She's a wonderful person, and I'm lucky to have her in my life."

"Are you sure you really know her? Do you know anything about her parents?"

Josh remembered that Alicia had mentioned that Dana's parents had passed away. "I know her parents are dead, but it's not her fault, and she's done well for herself."

"I'm still against it."

"Why? I've heard the other surgery attend-ings like her, her work ethic, and the way she cares for her patients. What exactly is it that you don't like about her?"

"What if she is interested in you for the money?"

Josh scoffed. "How would she know when I haven't told anyone about Grandma's will? Unless you've informed her, which I doubt very much since you've just found out today I have a girlfriend."

"And that's my point. Why am I just finding out you have a girlfriend? You could have told me before the blind date. You're lucky I managed to convince Alex Cunningham not to retaliate."

"How did you do that?"

"That's none of your business."

"Okay. Anyway, she's my girlfriend and that's that."

"I won't let you marry her!" his father growled.

Josh peered at his father. Seriously, why was he so angry about this? His eyes narrowed. "Is there something you are not telling me?"

His father looked away. "Nothing. She's just not the one for you," he said.

"Well, that's something you have to deal with, because she is staying in my life."

"We'll talk about this later," his father said. "You may go now."

Josh stormed out. Though he hated that his father hadn't agreed with him, maybe it was better this way. When they announced the broken engagement, his father would be relieved and wouldn't really dig to find out why they had gone their separate ways.

But all that would be moot if he couldn't get Dana to agree to the fake engagement. Her consent was central to the ruse working out.

It was time to put his powers of persuasion to good use.

CHAPTER 12

Dana rushed into the bathroom and shut the door behind her. Good thing it was only a couple steps away from the study. She leaned against the door and exhaled.

The atmosphere in the study had been tense, unlike what she had expected. And from the look of things, it was not the first time they'd had a heated argument. Who would have guessed Josh had a not-so-great relationship with his father?

Dana washed her hands in the sink, dried them, and fixed her hair. Now, she felt better and more prepared to face whatever was going on. She opened the bathroom door and stepped out. Loud voices were coming from the direction of the study.

"She's just not the one for you," his father said. She'd expected he might feel that way, but it still hurt. After all, he didn't really know her and hadn't even made the effort to do so.

"Well, that's something you have to deal with, because she is staying in my life," Josh said.

Warmth spread through Dana's chest at his words. She liked how Josh still stood up for her even though they weren't really dating. But having a fallout with his father for a fake relationship was not worth it.

But what was this whole business about getting married? Dana's nostrils flared. She hadn't consented to it, and she wanted no part of it. She would tell Josh that everything was over once he got out of the study.

"We'll talk about this later," his father said. "You may go now."

The study door creaked open and then shut. Josh strode down the hallway, his face a stormy whirlwind. He relaxed once he saw her.

"Dana, I'm so sorry you had to witness that," he said as he stopped in front of her.

She glared at him. "What was that all about?"

Josh ran a hand through his hair. "I'm sorry. I don't know what I was thinking when that popped out."

Well, if he thought looking cute would earn him a get-out-of-jail free card, he had another think coming. "You are sorry? Look, Josh, this is not what I signed up for. You need to go back in there and tell him the truth."

"Hold on for a second, Dana. I have a better proposition. How about we stay engaged 'til the end of the month?"

"What's this about an engagement? Josh, what's going through your head?"

"Dana, I'm sorry about the lies, but we can't unravel them just now. It would be disastrous to both you and me, and you know it."

True. It could wreck her career. Dana sighed. "How long are we talking about?"

"Maybe a few weeks."

"Are you kidding me?"

"Let me be honest with you. If this relationship breaks up any earlier than that, my father will be suspicious and the damage to your career would be the same as if we told him the truth now. But if we wait a few weeks and break up naturally, he won't think anything of it. He might even be happy given how opposed he is to the relationship. I also need your help to stay engaged by the end of this month for another reason."

"And what might that be?"

"Unfortunately, I can't tell you now. But my first point still stands, and that alone is enough for us to stay fake engaged. And my father is not the sort to go around talking about his family business, so this information shouldn't spread around town. This lying business is terrible, but I believe everything will work out in the end, okay?"

This was a real mess. But what could she do? "Okay, but only until the end of the month."

"Thanks, Dana."

Dana rubbed her eyes. This was not how she'd planned her day to go, but she couldn't cry over spilled milk. "I have to go."

"Can I have your number?"

"Whatever for?"

"Given that we are now engaged, it would be strange if we don't have each other's numbers.

And who knows what emergencies might crop up."

Josh had a point. "Give me your phone," she said. Josh handed his phone to her and she punched in her digits. "Here." She gave the phone back to him.

Josh fiddled with his phone, and Dana felt a buzz in her bag. "I just sent you a text with my number so you can save it," he said. "Can I drop you off?"

"No, I think you've done enough for today. I'll take a cab."

"Please let me call one for you." His warm light brown eyes pleaded with her, melting her insides and wearing down her defenses. Okay, she'd let him arrange a ride for her. But that didn't mean she'd forgotten what he'd done.

"Alright," she said.

Dana settled into the couch in her apartment and kicked off her shoes. Her feet hurt, and she rubbed them one after the other. Jasmine looked up from where she was reading on the living room floor. "You look nice. How was your date?" Jasmine said. Her gorgeous red hair was in a ponytail, and her lithe frame in her signature tank top and yoga pants.

Jasmine Banks was one of Dana's roommates, the other being Alicia Montgomery who was now engaged to Blake Dexington. Jasmine had escaped the fair skin gene as a redhead thanks to her mixed heritage and had a lovely olive tone instead. She was a third-year obstetrics and gynecology resident at Dexington Medical Center where they all worked. Jasmine's aunt owned the apartment they lived in, so it was a steal to rent.

Dana's forehead creased as she continued to massage her feet. "Don't even get me started. You won't believe what happened." Dana told her everything from how the blind date had started off to how they had ended up meeting Josh's father. Jasmine's mouth hung open by the time she was done. "Can you imagine meeting your departmental chair this way? This is just terrible!" Dana held her head in her hands.

"Are we talking about the same Josh, Blake's friend? The one that is popular with the nurses?"

"I forgot that bit. Don't even remind me."

"Well, congratulations on being engaged!"

Dana's head whipped up. "Are you kidding me? This isn't funny."

Jasmine flashed a big grin. "I mean think about it. You've done the impossible—acquiring a boyfriend and getting engaged on the same day." Dana grabbed a pillow from the couch and threw it at Jasmine's head. Jasmine laughed and dodged, the pillow hitting the coffee table. "But seriously, if he's best friends with Blake, he can't be that bad, and Alicia has only had good things to say about him. And don't tell me you didn't feel anything."

Dana ignored her latter comment. There was no way she was going to tell Jasmine that his touch, his voice, and his scent had made her skin tingle and turned her stomach to mush. "But this is fake. It's one thing to tell a blind date that you are his girlfriend, but it's a different ball-game altogether to do the same to his father, who just so happens to be my boss, so to speak. If this blows up, how can I face him or my colleagues? You know there's no way it wouldn't leak in the hospital if that happened. And what about my reputation? I've worked hard all these years and can't have everything go up in flames.

"How would I even finish my residency? Would I be able to get a fellowship spot here at Dexington Medical Center, especially since I need a recommendation from his father as part of the application process? You know how hard I've worked for this. I cannot afford to have everything get messed up. Besides, I'm not inter-ested in a relationship."

"But what if it's God's plan?"

Dana gave a nervous laugh. "That's impossible. God doesn't support lying. And there is no love in my future."

"You keep saying that, but are you sure? God can use any bad situation we create and work it out for our good. Maybe you need to keep your heart open. You never know."

"That's not going to happen." If only Jasmine knew. This conversation had to end here before Jasmine dug further. Besides, she was bone tired.

Dana yawned. "I'm exhausted. Good night." She got up and trudged up the stairs to her room on the second floor. Alicia also had a room on the same floor, while Jasmine occupied the master suite on the first floor.

"Don't worry. It's going to work out," Jasmine called after her.

Dana didn't think so. A relationship was not an option for her—Jasmine didn't know what she was talking about and had no idea.

She and Josh could never be an item no matter how much he affected her.

The truth about her made it impossible.

CHAPTER 14

Dana stretched and yawned as shards of light pierced the gaps between the floral curtains that hung over her windows. She'd had a fitful night's sleep as a result of all that happened yesterday. Good thing she wasn't on-call today. She was free for the most part unless an emergency happened and could laze around the apartment if she wanted, which was what she planned to do.

Engaged. It still seemed like a joke. What was Josh thinking yesterday to have blurted it out? She didn't really know much about him except what she had heard from Alicia, and learned of him the few times she had seen him when Alicia and Blake had all their friends together.

It was strange being engaged to someone she hadn't even dated, fake or not. Dana believed in only dating with the possibility of marriage and not just for the fun of it. Since marriage was not on her agenda, dates had been missing too from her schedule.

But sometimes she wished she could just date and marry like everyone else. It had been a dream of hers as a child and something she had looked forward to, until she'd found out the truth. She had been in a haze for a while and refused to believe it, but she'd eventually resigned herself to it. Now she lived vicariously through the soap operas she watched or through others like Alicia who had found love.

Dana burrowed further into her pillow. She'd been stunned when Alicia had confessed that her niece Willow was actually her daughter. Though the reasons Alicia had given had been logical, Dana had found it hard to understand how she could have done it.

But then she'd seen the real Alicia emerge and blossom after she'd met Blake, who had accepted everything about her, and it had made her realize how much hiding the truth had eaten and crushed much of who Alicia was. And Willow was a fantastic adorable girl.

Sometimes when she saw Blake and Alicia together, she wished she could find the kind of love they had. To find someone who could accept her wholeheartedly. But that was just a pipe dream. No man would want her if they really knew the truth.

But enough about that. She couldn't change what was. The only thing she could do was make the best of her life. And right now, that life included a fake engagement. Jake was very handsome, truth be told, and his voice, touch, and nearness affected her in a way no one else had.

Maybe she could live out a bit of her dream in this fake engagement, knowing it would eventually disappear. That way the memories of these weeks could keep her warm on those cold nights when it really hit her hard that she was all alone. For now, she would think about nothing else and just enjoy the experience.

Her phone rang on the bedside table. Dana reached out for it and looked at the screen. It was Linda. Probably calling to give her an earful about the date. If she ignored it, Linda would keep calling until she picked up. And that was not how she planned to spend this morning.

She pressed the green button. "Hello, Linda."

"Dana. Did I wake you?"

"No, you didn't." Dana sat up and settled against the headboard.

"I got a call from Ian last night about how your date went. I figured this morning might be a better time to find out what happened."

"Well, let's just say I wasn't keen on a guy who only talked about work, cars, and the family connections he had. I couldn't get a word in edgewise once he started. It was like listening to a lecture instead of a date."

Linda chuckled. "That bad?"

"Worse. He's a nice enough guy for those who like his type, but I'm not one of them."

"That sucks. I had hoped things would work out between both of you. But it seems it was not meant to be. Oh, and he mentioned you had a boyfriend. What was that all about?"

Dana grinned. This was the real reason Linda had called, yet she'd made it seem like an afterthought. "Well, I sort of have one."

"What do you mean sort of? You either have one or you don't."

Dana told her what had happened. She heard Linda gasp at the other end of the line. "Dana, I don't like the sound of this! This could blow up in your face, and you'd be the one to get hurt."

"I know. But everything happened so fast …"

"Give me his number. I need to call him and let him know that he can't mess with my baby girl."

Dana smiled. She knew Linda was protective of her, but it was always good to be reminded of it. "Don't worry, I'll be fine. If it gets bad, I will give you his number."

"Okay. I can't help being worried about you. But I will stay put since you've assured me you'll be okay. But my door is always open if you ever want to talk."

"Sounds good. I'll take you up on the offer if it comes to that."

"Hold on one second. I have a second call coming through."

Dana ran her hand through her hair and let out a big exhale. Linda had taken the news better than she had imagined. She could have rushed over or insisted on meeting Josh, which Dana didn't want.

Then Linda came back on the line. "Dana, it's my private investigator. Tammy O'Brien got into town last night and would like to meet you today at eleven a.m. She has a family emergency and will be out of town again for a couple of weeks and figured you would want to meet her as soon as possible. Since I know you have the day off, I went ahead and gave her the address of the café near your apartment. Can you make it?"

Dana's heart pounded in her chest. Maybe she would finally find out the truth about her mother's case.

"Dana, are you still there?" Linda asked with a worried tone.

Dana swallowed. "I'm fine. Yes, I can meet her. Thanks, Linda."

"Anytime. Unfortunately, I won't be able to make it, as I'm working today. There is an emergency fire we're trying to put out. But I'm sure you'll be fine meeting her alone. I'll catch up with you later about it."

"No worries, I'll be okay. Thanks, Linda. Talk to you later. Bye." The line went dead.

Dana dropped the phone on the bed and scrubbed her face with her hands. Her heart raced, and her legs shook as she tried to get out of bed. She sat back down on the edge of the bed and took a series of deep breaths. She'd been looking forward to this, but she hadn't known it would be today.

She took one last deep inhale and exhale and got up. She only had an hour to prepare and ready she would be.

She would not keep Tammy O'Brien waiting.

Dana entered the café and scanned the room. It was still too early for lunch break, but a few folks were already there—two young men in workout attire talked earnestly in a corner, a middle-aged woman with harried hair sipped from a coffee mug while staring out the window, and a young lady with pink spiked hair worked on a laptop, her headphones probably tuning out the noise in the room. The smell of roasted coffee mixed with tomato soup hung heavy in the air. Dana guessed the cooking staff were already prepping lunch.

Then she noticed a woman in her fifties—with mousy hair and freckles on her face—seated at the back of the room. Probably Tammy O'Brien. Dana headed in her direction and stopped in front of her. "Tammy O'Brien?" she asked.

The woman looked up. "Yes?"

"I'm Dana Adams. Mr. Roland, the investigator, said I would meet you here. About my mother's case."

"Please sit," Tammy said.

Dana slid into the nineteen-fifties style seat that was signature to the café. "Thank you for agreeing to meet with me."

"You're welcome. You look just like your mother."

Dana's pulse quickened. "Did you ever meet her?"

Tammy leaned back as she warmed her hands around the coffee mug she held. "Once. It was time for my lunch break at the medical records office, so I stopped by the ER to meet a friend of mine who was a nurse there. She wasn't at the nursing station, so I walked around to see if I could catch a glimpse of her.

"That's when I saw them working on your

mom, Sienna Adams. I remember her name because it was unusual, and the Sienna car was all the rave at the time. I'd even tried to save and buy one for driving to work, but it wasn't enough.

"She looked like she'd been in an accident, and they were doing everything to save her. I remember there was a young girl with startling blue eyes lying in the gurney next to hers, trying to reach her hand, though she had hurt her own stomach most likely in the same accident. I thought the girl was very brave. Those eyes stayed with me for many days, and it seems like they haven't changed." Her brown eyes searched Dana's face. "It was you, wasn't it?"

Dana nodded. "Do you remember anything else about the case? I've tried to get more information about how my mom died, but her case file was empty at the hospital."

Tammy took a sip of her coffee and nodded. "It's probably one of the files that was affected by the flooding of the basement that year."

"Flooding?" This was the first time Dana had heard about it.

"Yes. The hospital was still using a paper filing system at the time. So when one of the hospital pipes burst and flooded the basement, the medical records office was affected, and some of the writing in the case files got washed out. I'm guessing your mom's file was one of those that bore the brunt of it."

Dana's heart sank. It appeared the information was lost for good.

"But her file came across my table before the flooding, and I remembered the name. I'm not a nurse or doctor so most of the medical jargon didn't make sense to me."

Dana's heart rate picked up again. She leaned forward. "Was there anything you remember? Anything at all? Her death certificate said she died of traumatic shock."

"Yes, the file said she died of shock on the operating table."

Dana's head reeled with surprise. She'd heard nothing about it being a table death. This changed everything. Had someone's negligence gotten her mother killed? "Did it say why she went into shock?" she asked.

"I'm a little fuzzy on the details, but it was something about a rare blood disease that hadn't been diagnosed before she was taken to the operating room."

By now, Dana's heart pounded against her chest and she put her hands under the table so Tammy couldn't see they were shaking. "Can you remember the name of the blood disorder?"

Tammy shook her head. "It was some technical term I can't recall."

Hope seeped out of Dana's body and she slumped in her seat. She'd thought this would be it, the news that would shed more light.

"But have you asked the surgeon?" Tammy said.

Dana sat up straight. How could she forget about the surgeon? She leaned forward. "Do you remember who it was?"

"No. All I know was a nurse friend of mine had a crush on him. He was a popular surgeon at the time. I haven't seen her in years, but I can try and track down her information to see if she remembers him."

Dana grabbed Tammy's hand in hers. "I would be very grateful if you could do that. Thank you." And then she realized what she had done, and her cheeks warmed as she let go of Tammy's hand.

Tammy chuckled. "Don't worry, I understand. I would want to know everything too if it was my mother." She finished her cup of coffee. "I have to go now. I need to hit the road soon."

Dana fumbled in her jean pocket for her business card. "Here's my number on the back. Could you please give me a call as soon as you find out the name?"

Tammy took the card. "Sure. I'll let you know as soon as I do."

"Thank you so much. I really appreciate your help."

Tammy stood, and Dana did the same. "Anytime," Tammy said. "Oh, I remember there was a report in the file, something about the hospital looking into the death but finding nothing wrong with the surgery and treatment. It was standard procedure at the time for all deaths in the operating room."

Dana felt the tightness in her chest easing off. So it hadn't been negligence. She gave Tammy a smile of relief. "Thank you for telling me that."

Tammy's eyes searched her face. "Can I give you a piece of advice? The investigator mentioned you've been searching for more information about the case for quite some time. Maybe it's time to let go of the past. Your mother might want that for you as well."

Dana gave her a small smile in return but said nothing.

"Alright. Good luck, dear." Tammy picked up her purse and left the café.

Dana sat back down and let out a long exhale. "Thank you, God," she muttered.

The news had been different from what she'd expected. Her mother had died on the operating table, but it wasn't due to professional negligence. And she had a chance of finding out the name of the surgeon who had operated on her.

Surgeons never forgot table deaths, so it was very likely he would remember the name of the blood disorder. It was good news, more progress than she'd had in the last few years, and she couldn't wait to tell Linda.

She pulled out her phone from her jean pocket but noticed she already had an incoming call showing on the screen. It was an unknown number. She pressed the answer button. "This is Dana Adams."

"Hi, Dana. This is Celia Roman, Josh's mother."

Dana froze. Josh's mother? What was going on?

CHAPTER 15

*W*hy would Josh's mom be calling her? Dana hadn't met her yesterday at Josh's house, but she must have heard what happened.

"Hello?"

Dana swallowed the lump in her throat. She could do this. "Yes?"

"I thought I had lost you for a second." The voice sounded friendly. Maybe it wouldn't be as bad as she thought. "Would it be possible for you to meet me today, let's say at one p.m.?"

Dana looked at the time on her phone. It was twelve noon already. She could make it happen. "Sure."

"Wonderful, I'll text you the details. See you soon." The call ended.

Dana slumped back in her seat. Somehow, she'd forgotten Josh's mother in the whole mix. What was Dana supposed to do? See her or not see her? She had to admit she was curious about her. What kind of person was she? Would she turn up her nose at Dana since they were from money and she wasn't? Josh would know.

She sat up straight. She had to tell him about this. He would know what to do. She scrolled through her phone for his number, which she had saved before going to bed last night and dialed it. It rang for a while and then went to voicemail. She dialed again. Why wasn't he picking up? It went again to voicemail, so she left a message.

So now what? Dana scratched her head. Blake might know how to reach Josh, but it would be awkward asking him, and she didn't know if Josh had told him anything.

Her phone buzzed and she looked at the screen. It was a text message from Josh's mother to meet her at the Windsor floor of the Waterbridge Mall.

Dana had heard about the place. It was the

exclusive shopping floor for the ultra-rich! Why meet there? Since she couldn't reach Josh, she had no pointers on what that meant as far as his mom was concerned.

Dana bit her lip and tossed her phone on the table. *Guess what? I can do this*, Dana thought. It wasn't like she was going into the lion's den. Even if she was, she had nothing to be afraid of.

She lifted her chin. She would go. She had nothing to fear, and it wasn't like they were in a real relationship. And she would make sure she looked her best. All the fashion magazines she'd flipped through daily since she was a teenager would come to good use in choosing the right outfit. She had nothing to lose from looking good. Suddenly, one hour didn't seem long enough.

She grabbed her phone off the table and strode out of the café.

Time to go impress a fake mother-in-law-to-be.

"What are you doing?" Jasmine stood at the door of Dana's room and peeked in.

"I'm getting ready for a date, and I'm looking for what to wear." Dana rifled through her wardrobe. She was looking for a royal blue A-line dress that she'd bought at a sale a couple of weeks ago and had tucked away until she found the right occasion for it. Today's appointment was it.

"Ah! Found it," Dana said. She tried on the outfit. The designer dress complemented her eyes, and paired with her favorite cream-colored military-style knee-length spring jacket and a pair of nude pumps, she would fit right in with the mall's clientele.

"A date? With Josh?" Jasmine entered the room and sat at the edge of the bed.

"No. With his mother." Dana ran a pinkish-tinged lip gloss over her lips and dabbed a bit of blush on her cheeks.

"Wait! When did that happen?"

"About thirty minutes ago. And I can't reach Josh, so I'm going. Might as well get it over with and look good while doing so." Dana straightened and twirled herself around to see her reflection in the full-length wall mirror.

"Girl, you look hot!"

Dana grinned. "I have to. I'm going to the Windsor floor."

Jasmine looked up. "The Windsor floor at the Waterbridge Mall?"

"One and the same."

"Make sure you remain confident and look everyone in the eye."

Dana glanced at Jasmine. "Have you been there?"

Jasmine looked down and appeared more interested in the block design of Dana's duvet. "Sort of. Anyway, don't let anyone intimidate you. Be yourself."

Dana gazed down at Jasmine's head of hair. There was something Jasmine wasn't telling her. But this was not the time to pursue it. She couldn't afford to be late.

She picked up her nude oversized clutch purse from her bed and tucked it under her arm. "I'll see you later," Dana said.

She strode out of her room.

Dana stepped out of the cab and walked through the ground floor of the Waterbridge Mall.

Saturday was prime shopping day, and the mall was no exception as a destination. Shoppers were everywhere with carts piled high with shopping bags, and even dogs were not left out. It seemed one in every five shoppers either had a chihuahua in their arms or peeking out of a doggy diaper bag.

Dana headed toward the marble concierge desk situated near the elevators. "Hello, how do I get to the Windsor floor?" she asked the lady in a blue and white uniform whose blonde hair was pulled into a smooth chignon.

The lady flashed her a perfect smile. "Do you have an appointment, ma'am?"

"Yes, with Mrs. Roman," she said.

"May I have your name and your driver's license please?" the lady asked her.

"It's Dana Adams." Dana pulled out her driver's license from her clutch and handed it over. She'd barely managed to get one. The experience had been traumatic—it had reminded her too much of her mother's accident. She'd never bothered to drive again, and it had been easy renewing it online whenever it was set to expire. She appreciated having the license as a government approved ID but nothing more.

The lady looked up something on a computer and then swiped the ID through a machine which spat out a mall identification badge. The lady handed both the license and badge back to Dana. "Please swipe the tag against the card reader once you get into the elevator, and then press the top floor button. That should take you to the Windsor floor. Have a good day, ma'am." The lady flashed her another smile.

Dana nodded. "Thank you." She slipped her license back into her purse and made her way to the elevators.

She followed the lady's instructions once she was inside, and the elevator doors closed as expected. Dana took a deep breath as she opened her coat buttons and leaned against the elevator railing. It wasn't like she was going for an interview, only a date with Josh's mother.

She shut her eyes briefly. But who was she kidding? She was terrified. This whole situation wasn't real, and it was Josh's mother for goodness sake. Even if she had no relationship with Josh, she was still Prof. Roman's wife. She had to make sure she didn't offend her no matter what.

The elevator pinged, and Dana opened her eyes. She hadn't even noticed when it had stopped moving. She smoothed down her dress and stepped out. A concierge stood waiting for her by the elevator. "This way, ma'am," the lady said before leading her through one of many sets of double doors into a massive room filled with large couches arranged in a semi-circle.

As she got closer, six pairs of eyes looked back at her. These ladies resting on the couches looked like they had just stepped out of a magazine.

Dana felt cold sweat break out on her skin. What was going on? She was only supposed to be meeting Josh's mom.

One of the women, a stunning woman who looked much younger than her age with strawberry-blonde hair cut into a stylish bob and captivating grey eyes got up and walked up to her, a welcoming smile on her face. "There you are. Hello, Dana." She pulled her into a hug. "I'm Celia, Josh's mom," she whispered into Dana's ear. "Sorry to meet you like this, but the news has already spread through town." She straightened and pulled Dana's hand. "Come.

Let me introduce you." She led Dana to the couch she'd been sitting on.

Dana sat down, keeping a set smile on her face as Celia introduced her to the other women. These were all members of Dexington's elite and were movers and shakers in their own right. Dana recognized one or two of them that she had seen on TV before. "The only person missing is Sarah Dexington, and she doesn't come very often," Josh's mother said as she concluded the introductions. Ah, Blake's mother. From what Dana had heard of her, she could guess this wasn't really her kind of scene.

The woman who Celia had introduced as Pauline Cunningham, Alex Cunningham's wife, tapped her perfectly manicured finger against her knee as she scrutinized Dana. "I heard you are engaged to Josh," she said in an affected tone.

Dana peered at her. She had a striking resemblance to Josh's date. Maybe she was her mother. Then little wonder she didn't seem to like Dana. She probably felt that Dana had snatched Josh away from her daughter. Dana remembered what Jasmine had said, and she lifted her eyes to meet hers. "Yes, we are dating."

Pauline looked at Celia with a raised brow. "But that's not what I heard," Pauline said. "So she is just passing through. So why all the fuss?" Some of the other women chuckled and color rose on Celia's face.

Dana's blood boiled. She'd just met Josh's mom, but no one had the right to talk to her that way. She plastered a sweet smile on her face. "Oh, we are dating, but we are already talking about engagement, babies, and stuff." She flashed an encouraging smile at Celia. Pauline's face paled, and the other women who'd supported her averted their eyes in embarrassment.

"So what do you do for a living?" one of the other ladies asked.

"I'm a fourth-year general surgery resident at Dexington Medical Center. I'm looking to specialize in vascular surgery."

The ladies all nodded their heads as if impressed. But Pauline Cunningham gave her a disapproving glance instead.

"What about your parents?" Pauline asked.

"They are dead," Dana said. The atmosphere

was thick with silence at her response. It didn't matter. Even though her parents were no more, she was proud of them and she didn't need to prove it to anyone.

Celia rushed to her rescue. "But she attended all the best schools and without needing scholarships. That could only mean her parents made adequate arrangements for her care."

Dana gave Celia a sharp look. How had she known that? Had they done a background check on her? Maybe Josh's father had discussed her; some of that information was in her residency application package. She had no bones to pick with Celia since she was only trying to help.

Pauline pretended to yawn. "All this talk is boring." She snapped her fingers, and three ladies in mall uniforms appeared, each pulling a rack full of clothes behind them. They stopped the racks in front of the couch area and then stepped away. Pauline turned to Dana, "Dana, could you pick out an outfit that would suit Celia? Hope you don't mind, Celia dear," she said in a false honeyed tone.

Dana hid a smile. So Pauline meant to trap her. Too bad she didn't know Dana loved to stay up to date with all the current trends in the fashion world.

She got up and walked over to the racks and took a quick look over the clothes. She sorted them into three groups and then turned to address the ladies. "The first batch includes last season's items, the middle ones either don't suit Celia's wonderful coloring or don't work for this season. And the last two items on the third rack would work well for any of the charity events Mrs. Roman loves to engage in." Good thing Alicia had mentioned once in their conversations how much Josh's mom loved philanthropic work.

Celia beamed with pride, and the other women gave her envious smiles. Pauline struggled to hold back her anger.

"I think we've taken too much of your time, Dana," said the lady who had been introduced as the mayor's wife. "As a surgeon, I'm sure you are already busy enough as it is saving lives. It was great meeting you, and I hope to see more of you in the future." The other women murmured their assent.

"It was great meeting you all," Dana responded.

Celia got up. "Come, Dana, let me walk you out." They walked in silence to the elevators where Celia pressed the elevator button and then hugged her. "Thank you," she whispered and then straightened.

"It was nice to meet you, Mrs. Roman," Dana said.

"Please call me Celia. I look forward to seeing more of you. Don't be a stranger."

Dana smiled and nodded.

The elevators arrived, and the doors opened. Dana entered, turned, and gave her a small wave. Celia waved back and then the doors shut.

Dana sagged against the elevator railing. That had been nerve-wracking. Thankfully, it was all over. It wasn't what she had expected, but she'd held her own, and Celia had seemed pleased. Mission accomplished.

Dana stepped out of the elevators on the ground floor and strode through the mall exit. As she looked around for the cab stand, her phone rang. It was Josh. She answered the call. "This is Dana."

"Hey, Dana. It's Josh."

"Where have you been?" she growled at him.

"I got paged for an emergency trauma case earlier today, so I just got out of the OR and heard your voicemail. You met with my mother? Did she call you?"

"Yes. I met her with her friends."

"Oh, the Wonder Six." What was Josh talking about? "The women who hold the keys to the city," Josh finished with a bemused tone.

"Well, it wasn't funny. It was almost like being interrogated, and Mrs. Cunningham seemed to have something against me."

"I bet. That's my blind date's mom."

"I guessed as much."

"I'm almost certain she was the one that brought up your name. My mom wouldn't have raised it since she hadn't had a chance to talk to me first about the engagement. Sorry you had to go through that," Josh said in an apologetic tone. "I should have run interference for you. I'll make sure to speak with my mother."

It was so hard to stay mad at him when he was like this. "It's alright. Your mom was a darling."

"That's a first. I've never heard her described that way."

"Anyway, pick up your calls next time."

Dana clasped her hand over her mouth. Oops. Who said there would be a next time? There was no way she was planning to call him more in the future. She hoped he didn't think she had a crush on him or anything.

"Yes, ma'am. I'll do so *next* time."

Dana's face heated up. Now Josh would think she was into this fake relationship when she wasn't. "I have to go." She pressed the end button.

Sheesh, what was wrong with her? This was just a fake relationship, nothing more.

There couldn't be anything more than that.

CHAPTER 16

osh shook his head in wonder as he stretched out his legs in front of him. He was in the surgical call room working on the notes for his second emergency surgery of the day. The patient was a college football star who had needed emergency ACL repair to preserve his chances of being able to play again. Though the surgery had gone well, he would still be out of commission for a few months and would miss the rest of the football season.

Josh chuckled. He had just ended a call with his mother, who had gushed with praise about Dana and especially how she had impressed her friends. Apparently, Dana had won over the

Wonder Six. A true miracle if there ever was one. How had she done it? The Wonder Six were known to be hard to please and rarely ever gave their stamp of approval. Yet, Dana had gotten it.

Now he wanted to know more about her. She'd piqued his interest for sure with the way her blue eyes seemed to reach into his soul and with the little sparks of electricity that buzzed on his skin at her touch. However, that was nothing.

But winning over the Wonder Six? That was a whole new level of awesomeness. Apparently, there was more to Dana than met the eye. And his mother wasn't helping matters with the not-so-subtle hints she kept dropping about making sure he didn't mess things up with Dana. He'd never seen his mother take to anyone so quickly.

He crossed his arms over his chest and leaned back in the chair. Dana, Dana. What magic was she working? She looked quiet and delicate on the outside but was a tiger on the inside. And why was thinking about her making him feel these unnamed sensations?

He had to watch himself. She could quickly mess him up if he wasn't careful. But he still wanted to get to know her more. He could do that as a friend, right? And it would really help to make their relationship more believable, come to think of it. Getting to know her and getting into a relationship were two separate things, so he had nothing to lose. It wasn't like he was planning to open his heart.

Theirs was only a pretend relationship, nothing more. He couldn't afford to be shackled down after coming out from under his father's thumb, which would happen once he received his grandma's inheritance.

An unbidden image of Dana standing like Joan of Arc in front of the Wonder Six rose in his mind's eye and he chuckled.

"What's funny?" Josh looked up to see Stan enter the call room. Josh hadn't even heard him open the door.

"Nothing," Josh said.

Stan pulled out another chair from the table and sat down. "You have a strange look in your eye. What's going on?"

There was no way Josh was going to tell him about Dana unless he wanted the story to spread around the hospital like wildfire. Stan was a sieve when it came to anything about relation-ships. He could even attribute it to the non-existent bet that he'd proposed, one that Josh had clearly not agreed to. Though the relationship was fake, he still felt protective about it. So he changed the topic. "Are you done with Mr. Williams?" he asked.

Stan grimaced. "Now I see why you didn't protest when I took over his care," he accused in mock anger.

"He is interesting," Josh said with a smile.

"That's all you can say? The man almost killed me with his demands!"

Josh laughed out loud. That was typical Mr. Williams.

Stan looked at him quizzically. "I haven't seen you laugh like this since orientation on the first day of residency."

No way was he going there with Stan. Time to end the conversation before Stan grilled him further. Josh got up. And it was really time to go home and rest. Hopefully, there would be no more emergency calls for the rest of the day.

"I'm out," he said and strode toward the door.

"Hey! Are you going to be at Blake's mini-golf tournament?" Stan called out.

Oh shoot! He'd forgotten about it. Blake

Dexington, his best friend, loved to put together events now and then for his friends to hang out and de-stress. Josh had spoken to him two days ago and he'd sounded tired, which wasn't surprising since he was finishing up his residency while preparing to take over his father's role as the CEO & Chairman of Dexington Healthcare. Blake's father was retiring as a result of the mini-stroke he'd suffered a few months ago.

But Blake had perked up as soon as they'd started talking about the event. This time it was at an indoor golf range, and Blake had booked the whole place. Josh expected it to be lots of fun.

Since Alicia was going to be there, there was a good chance that Dana would be too, and he could learn more about her that way. So, of course he'd be there. But he didn't need to tell Stan that.

So Josh gave him a wave over his head and left the room.

CHAPTER 17

Dana kicked off her heels as she closed the door to their apartment. She was beyond exhausted and just wanted to fall into bed and take a long nap. She looked around the space that shared an open concept floor plan with the dining room and kitchen, and which boasted grand bay windows, a fireplace, crown molding, and a winding staircase that led to the upper floors.

She loved their little abode and the wonderful people she shared it with. She'd never had close friends before, not even when she was in college, but her roommates, Alicia and Jasmine, had become more than that—they were like the sisters she'd never had.

Alicia had gotten engaged to Blake a few months ago and was now busy planning her upcoming wedding while juggling a busy residency schedule. She wasn't around as much anymore. Alicia's niece-turned-daughter, Willow, had been discharged from the hospital and had needed a live-in nanny to take care of her and shuttle her to and from school. So Alicia had rented a bigger apartment closer to Willow's school. But she still dropped by once a week to have dinner and catch up with Jasmine and Dana.

It was still surreal that Willow was attending school, but she had insisted on a normal school experience after being a cystic fibrosis inpatient for most of her life, and Alicia had agreed. So far, the decision had been a good one—Willow was thriving and had even become popular in school. It was hard to believe she was the same person who had been at death's door a few months ago. Thank goodness for advances in medicine and clinical trials—one of which had saved Willow's life.

Dana was happy for Alicia. She had found love and totally deserved it. She, on the other hand, couldn't have that—no one wanted a broken person. But since she couldn't do anything about it, she would put it out of her mind. And what better way than with ice cream.

She padded to the kitchen and opened the freezer. Yes! Chocolate fudge ice cream. Just what she needed.

"How was your date?" Dana whirled around to see Jasmine leaning against the kitchen counter in black yoga pants and a light blue sleeveless top, her luscious flaming hair cascading in waves around her. Jasmine always appeared laid back, but she was the most dedicated grab-the-bull-by-the-horns kind of girl that Dana had ever met. And she never failed to turn heads, though Dana had never seen her show an interest in any guy.

"You scared me! I didn't know you were home."

Jasmine sat on one of kitchen stools. "I changed my mind about going out today. How did it go?"

"I think it went well."

Jasmine's eyes twinkled. "Details, girl, details!"

Dana grabbed one of the other stools and sat down. Jasmine could be like a pit bull sometimes. Dana might as well give up and save the time. So she told Jasmine everything that had happened at the mall. "So his mom was nice and the Wonder Six, as Josh called them, seemed okay," she finished.

Jasmine leaned her elbows on the kitchen countertop. "I'm amazed, Dana. Trust me, those ladies are hard to please."

"You know them?"

"Who doesn't? I'm surprised you hadn't heard of them."

"Anyway, I'm glad it turned out well. His mom was great, not what I expected considering how formal his dad is."

"I don't think formal is the right way to describe him. I would say stiff and full of—"

"Stop it! He's not that bad. He's just really into his orthopedic surgery world."

"Yeah? Too high for mere mortals like us? See, you are already defending his family, or should I say your family."

Dana touched the back of her hand against Jasmine's forehead. "Are you okay? Because that's the only reason you would be saying all this rubbish."

Jasmine playfully knocked away Dana's

hand. "I thought you were being serious for a moment there." She tapped her fingers on the kitchen countertop. "So are you going to be at Blake's mini-golf tournament tomorrow?"

Dana fiddled with the cover of the ice cream pint. "Yes, I plan to be there."

Jasmine leaned forward, a cheeky grin on her face. "And Josh is going to be there."

Dana's cheeks warmed. "I guess so."

"Dana, when are you going to stop pretending? You obviously like Josh."

Her face warmed. "I don't know what you are talking about."

"See? Even your body is telling me the truth."

"Seriously, it's only a fake relationship, nothing more."

"Isn't that what Alicia said, yet she is marching down the aisle in a few months to marry Blake? Give love a chance. You like him, and his mom likes you. You are all set!"

"Stop it!"

"Okay, okay. Now when are you going to stop playing with that ice cream cover and open it for us to eat?"

CHAPTER 18

Josh arrived early for the tournament, which was scheduled to start at noon. He'd convinced himself it was only to warm up his rusty skills, but his eyes kept searching for the cute blonde hair among the sea of friends that hung around the course.

He felt a slap on his back that made him stumble, and he turned to see Blake grinning from ear-to-ear. "I've been calling your name, but you seemed preoccupied. Dana hasn't arrived."

"Who said that's who I was looking for?"

Blake laughed. "Hey, man, I've known you for a long time and I know that look."

"What—"

That was when Josh heard the voice that was uniquely hers, the one he refused to admit to himself that he had been dreaming about for the past few days. He turned to see Dana looking cute in a white mini-skort paired with a pink and white golf shirt. She looked breathtaking, and Josh couldn't take his eyes off her.

He knew the moment she saw him. She stopped speaking mid-sentence but quickly got a hold of herself and turned back to her friends like nothing had happened.

Josh grinned, his attention focused solely on her. He barely heard what Blake said before he moved away. So this was the game she wanted to play?

Well, he was more than happy to oblige.

CHAPTER 19

D ana hadn't expected to see Josh as soon as she walked into the indoor golf course. He looked yummy enough to eat in his grey and white striped golf shirt paired with white shorts that enhanced the amber flecks of his eyes.

Her heart rate quickened. She had to get a grip of herself. It was only a pretend arrangement. So she turned back to her conversation with Jasmine and Lilly, a fellow resident from the hospital, though she barely heard what they said.

It was almost time for the tournament to start, and she needed to practice. This wasn't a game she had played before, but Alicia had assured her it was easy to learn. Jasmine had given her an overview and a few pointers, so she hoped she wouldn't do too badly today.

She spotted an empty lane in the practice area and walked over to it. She picked a ball from the small basket set near the head of the lane. Dana placed the ball on the tee and swung the putter like Jasmine had taught her. But she missed. She positioned herself again to take another swing.

"You need to straighten your back and keep your form loose," the voice that did strange things to her insides said from behind her.

Dana felt Josh's hands snake over hers from behind and electricity shot through her. His spicy mint aftershave made her senses tingle, and warmth radiated through her body. She was tempted to step away from him, but she had to admit she was enjoying his closeness at the same time.

"I need you to concentrate," he said in an amused tone. Dana's ears warmed. But then she stiffened her spine. How dare he laugh at her? She would show him that she wasn't affected by him.

Dana looked down at the ball in concentration, leveled her breathing, and then swung the club. It made contact with the ball, which rolled ahead in a straight line before landing into the hole.

Dana shrieked and hugged Josh. A hole-in-one on her first stroke! A grin split her face. What a way to start her practice! That was when she noticed the surprised look on Josh's face and her arms around him. What was she thinking? She dropped her hands so quickly, like she had been burned, but not before he looped his arms around her and pulled her in.

Dana's eyes were drawn to his face, and her breath hitched. Was Josh going to kiss her? His eyes searched hers as if asking for permission before he leaned toward her, his spicy mint scent washing over her senses. She didn't resist and waited with bated breath. She saw his eyes flick down to her lips. She was supposed to move away, but for some reason she felt immobile, hypnotized under his gaze.

Dana's heart pounded. Josh leaned forward, pulling her closer until there was hardly any space between them …

"There you are," Blake's voice intruded, and Dana jumped back and out of Josh's arms. Her face grew warm, and she looked away while running her hands down her outfit. What had she been thinking? How could she have almost kissed Josh with all these people around?

"Hello, Dana," Blake said. Dana just nodded and fiddled with her club. She wished the ground would just open and she would disappear.

Blake grabbed Josh's arm. "Excuse us for one second," he said to Dana. "We'll be right back." Then he dragged Josh away.

Dana watched them go. What was that all about?

"You so like him," a familiar voice said from her side.

Dana yelped and jumped. "Jasmine, you scared me!" she said.

Jasmine laughed. "You were totally into that almost kiss."

Dana covered her face—still holding the club—and groaned. She was sure her face was almost as red as a tomato.

"Are you sure there's nothing between you two?" Jasmine asked.

"Nothing. We are just friends.," Dana muttered into the hands that covered her face.

"If that was *nothing*, I wonder what *something* would look like."

"Oh, stop it!" Dana lifted the club threateningly.

"Okay, okay," Jasmine lifted her hands in mock surrender. "But Dana, there is nothing wrong with this. Just take your time and get to know him."

"Thank you for the wonderful advice, but I won't. There is no need."

"If you say so," Jasmine said with a lingering smile. "Now, let's go watch some cute boys play golf," she said with a twinkle in her eye.

Dana laughed, picked up her golf bag, and followed her.

CHAPTER 20

"Hey, why did you pull me away?" Josh ripped Blake's hand from his arm.

"You were like a tiger about to eat his prey. Can't you see where we are? The whole rumor would be around town by the end of the day."

Josh ran his hand through his hair. Blake had a point. He could not allow anything to harm Dana's reputation. Especially when she was only doing him a favor. But he hadn't been able to help himself. When she hugged him, he'd lost his head and had wanted to kiss her, even though he didn't have the right to do so.

"Josh, you shouldn't kiss her unless you are

sure you want to turn this relationship from fake to real. Don't send her mixed signals."

"I know, I know. I just forgot myself in that moment."

"Well, get it together," Blake said. "Have you considered you might truly like her?"

The thought had crossed Josh's mind, but he wasn't sure if he could explore it. Wouldn't the relationship cage him—the one thing he didn't want right now?

"Josh, having a relationship can be liberating, not binding, if you find the love of your life. Alicia is the best thing that ever happened to me, and you could have that too if you give love a chance."

Maybe Blake had a point. Blake had never been one to lie to him. And Blake's parents, and now Blake, had great relationships. But they were both father and son. Was it possible for him too even though he was his father's son? Could he take a chance? It was something to think about.

"Anyway, keep your hands to yourself 'til you make up your mind," Blake said.

"Thanks."

"Don't worry. That's what friends are for."

Blake slapped him on the back. "Have I told you we have fittings next week?"

"Fittings?"

"For the tuxes."

"Wait, isn't that too early?"

"That's what Alicia wants. And what she wants, she gets. I'll text you the address and time."

"You are a goner."

"Wait until you meet the love of your life, and you'll practically become putty in her hands. You'll love it too."

An image of Dana rose in Josh's mind, and he brushed it away. Oh man, he was in trouble if every discussion made him think of her. Time to shift gears.

"Let's go play some golf," he said.

CHAPTER 21

Dana lay on her bed and tucked the duvet around her. The air outside was a bit chilly and seemed to permeate the house despite the central heating.

The mini-golf tournament had been so much fun, and it had been great catching up with Alicia and Willow. She'd only caught glimpses of Josh here and there, like he'd made an effort to avoid her. She and Jasmine had only arrived back home about an hour ago.

Once she'd taken a hot shower, Dana had logged into the electronic medical records to see which patients had been admitted to her team over the weekend and to read up on their case notes. Tomorrow promised to be a grueling day with all the new patients to follow up and surgeries planned. It was best to go to bed as early as possible so that she would be well rested for the next day.

But sleep refused to come. It was like her mind was still playing a loop of the almost kiss. She hadn't intended to hug Josh, but it had seemed so natural to do so, and for some reason, she hadn't minded it or the almost kiss.

Could she be falling for Josh? Honestly, she didn't know. It could be the effect of the pretend relationship, or it could truly be something real between them. But she wasn't sure which one it was.

But one thing was clear: Dana Adams was open to exploring the possibility of a relationship with Josh. Dana knew enough of herself to know that she wouldn't have been willing to allow the kiss if her heart hadn't already reached that conclusion. She wasn't sure if anything would come of it, and she still believed that she was not meant for love, but her heart wouldn't let her have peace until she tried to get to know Josh Roman and what made him tick.

Her phone rang. Dana looked at the screen

and sat up. It was Josh. Talk about good timing. She pressed the answer button. "Hello."

"Hi, Dana." Her stomach melted at the sound of his voice. She was definitely in trouble.

"Hi, yourself," Dana responded.

"What are you up to?"

"Just chilling."

"Me too." There was a pause on the line. "Hey, would you like to go out to dinner with me tomorrow?"

Dana's heart pounded. This was it. Time to put herself out there. She swallowed. "I'm not sure."

"What do you mean?"

"Tomorrow's schedule looks tight. I don't know when I'll be done for the day."

Josh chuckled. "You had me there for a second. I thought you meant you weren't sure you wanted to go out to dinner with me."

"Oh."

"How about this? Why don't I call you at six p.m. tomorrow to find out if you can make it? If not, we'll just cancel and reschedule for another day."

"That should work."

"Okay, I'll call you tomorrow. Good night,

Dana." The whisper of her name on his lips sounded so sweet and special.

"Good night." The call ended.

Dana flopped back on her bed and squealed into her pillow. She couldn't help being excited. She was going out on a date! *You know it won't lead anywhere,* a voice whispered in her head. But she didn't care anymore. Nothing said she couldn't enjoy the time with Josh while it lasted. Even if this relationship remained fake, she would still enjoy this and keep it as a memory.

She needed a new dress.

Lunchtime tomorrow was now shopping hour.

CHAPTER 22

"You look delicious," Jasmine said as Dana stood before the mirror to examine herself.

"You think so? Wait! … What?"

"You look beautiful enough to eat."

"Jasmine, you are crazy."

Jasmine chuckled. "I just like to tease you."

"Seriously though, do you think this dress is okay?" Dana said as she smoothed down the princess blue sheath dress paired with black pumps and tights.

"You look great. I'm sure Josh won't take his eyes off you the whole time."

Dana's face grew warm. "Stop teasing me."

Jasmine grinned and then cocked her head. "I think I hear a car."

Josh had called as promised, and Dana had confirmed that she could make the date. So they had agreed that he would come and pick her up from home at seven p.m.

The doorbell rang through the house. Dana and Jasmine looked at each other.

"I think he's here," Jasmine said. "Have fun on your date and save all the juicy details for me." Jasmine winked and walked down the stairs to her room.

Dana slipped a black spring jacket over her dress and grabbed her clutch. She took a deep breath before walking down the stairs to the front door. She opened it to see Josh in a grey fitted sports jacket with a matching pocket square, worn over a blue-striped button-down shirt and paired with tan slacks and custom Italian shoes. He was a sight for sore eyes. Jasmine was wrong. Josh was the one who looked good enough to eat.

"Hi Dana." An appreciative smile creased his face. "You look beautiful."

Dana smiled. "Thank you. You don't look bad yourself."

"Are you all set?"

"I'm ready." Dana closed the door behind her and walked down the steps with Josh. 'Where are we going?"

"It's a surprise. I think you'll love it."

Josh led Dana to a black gleaming sports car with a Bugatti logo on the grill. She knew Josh's parents were wealthy, but a Bugatti was a very expensive car. How could he afford it?

Josh opened the passenger door for her, and Dana stepped in. The car's black and white interior was even more luxurious with a white Chiron logo stitched into the quilted black leather seats that molded around Dana's frame.

Josh walked over to the other side and slid into the driver's seat.

"Nice car," Dana said.

"Thanks. It was a gift from my grandmother," he said as if he'd read her earlier thoughts.

Dana hoped Josh was a good driver—she hated speed driving of any form. "What kind of driver are you—slow, medium, fast?" she asked.

Josh peered at her. "It depends." What did that even mean? "Why do you want to know?"

"I'm kind of leery of fast driving of any kind."

"Don't worry. I practice safe driving in every situation. You'll be fine."

Dana hoped it was true, because it could put an end to the date pretty fast.

This was one area she would never compromise.

Josh got Dana safely to the restaurant as promised. He'd driven at a moderate speed and after a few minutes, Dana had finally relaxed and enjoyed the ride. This was the first time in many years she felt comfortable enough in a car to not jump out of the vehicle as soon as it halted.

The maître d led them to their table in the swanky restaurant, and Josh pulled out the chair for Dana to sit down.

"This is a beautiful restaurant," Dana said as she looked around. "I've never been here." The restaurant boasted a classy old-world interior with ornate chandeliers and a comforting ambience reminiscent of Asian serenity.

"It's a Thai fusion restaurant that just opened recently. The food is spectacular and in so much demand that you have to call a month in advance to make reservations."

"So how did you get a table? I'm pretty sure we hadn't really met a month ago," Dana said with a tease in her voice.

"My family knows the chef," Josh said cryptically.

The guy sitting across from her had such connections. They were really in separate social circles—he came from wealth and money, while she was … well an orphan.

An awkward silence elapsed between them. Thankfully, a waiter arrived to take their orders, bringing warm white fluffy bread served with a panda custard dip.

"What would you like?" Josh asked Dana.

"Whatever you think is great here. I'm not picky about food."

"Good to know. Why don't I order different dishes and we can split them?"

Hmmm. A man after her own heart. Just like what she and Linda would do. "Sounds good to me."

Josh turned to their waiter and rattled off

their order. It was obvious that he'd been here before. The waiter left with their order.

Dana bowed her head to pray and then took a bite of the dip-coated bread. It was sooo good. The custard's creamy coconut flavor married well with the vanilla-like flavor of the scented pandan leaf extract in the dip. She could have eaten everything off the plate, but she held herself back for what was sure to come.

Dana noticed Josh's eyes on her, and her face grew warm. "Is there something on my face?" she asked.

"I like when a woman appreciates good food," he said.

"Why, thank you," Dana responded with a smile.

"So, Dana, what's your favorite movie?"

Dana leaned back into her chair. "I would say *Gone with the Wind*. What about you?"

"*Something about Mary*."

Dana burst out laughing. "Are you serious?"

"Do I look like I'm joking? I just like it. I don't buy into that whole 'girls must like chick flicks and guys must like action movies' thing. For your information, I don't particularly care for action movies. I do like thrillers, but most of the time I prefer something light and fluffy. Life is already too serious as it is."

Dana couldn't believe what she was hearing. Josh was the first man she'd met that liked chick flicks. And he hadn't been afraid to let her know. Hmmm. A man comfortable in his own skin.

"And I also watch soap operas," Josh said.

Dana gasped. Would the surprises never end? "Are you serious? I'm also a big fan of them."

"Really? That's great. I got hooked from watching them with my grandma. But I don't really watch a lot now given how busy my schedule is. But I have a huge collection at home. I could show you what I have."

"I would like to see them and we can compare notes. What else do you like? Books?"

"I'm not a big fan of non-fiction books. I know, strange right, given the profession that we are in? But I like epic fantasy novels."

"Have you read Ted Henderson's books?"

"Every one of them."

Dana took a sip of her water. "Even the latest copy? I can't wait for it to come out."

"I already have a copy," Josh replied with a twinkle in his eye.

Dana choked on her drink. "How is that even possible? I know he doesn't do ARCs."

Josh grinned. "It's a secret."

"Can I read it? Pretty please?" She batted her eyelashes at him.

Josh burst out laughing. "Okay, I'll stop by my place after dinner if you like and give it to you."

"Thank you!"

The dinner service arrived and did not disappoint. They spent the next thirty minutes making small conversation and enjoying the food—plates of juicy chicken marinated in Thai flavors, minced beef simmered in hot Thai sauce that melted in her mouth, grilled octopus served with a signature seafood sauce that was the right mix of crunch and spice, and classic Thai broad noodles served in a savory broth.

Each dish was delicious and Dana was filled to bursting by the time they were done. This was one restaurant that was worth a repeat, and Dana resolved to bring Linda here soon.

Their conversation was enlightening. Josh was very easy to talk to. Dana found out he was crazy about soccer and even part-owner of a European soccer club. And his dream was to open soccer clinics all over the country in under-privileged areas so kids with an interest in soccer would not only have a place to learn the sport and make their dreams come true, but receive two good meals a day and medical care if needed.

"It's how some of the soccer clubs in Europe are structured, and I've seen how successful it can be. I want it for the kids here in this country," Josh finished.

"Wow, that's such an ambitious dream. Won't it take lots of money?"

"It would. I'm working on it. I also don't expect everything to happen at once. I plan to start small and expand it over time."

"So does this mean you are planning to specialize in a sports orthopedic fellowship?"

Josh's face tightened. "Not really."

"Why? That would be a natural fit."

Josh kept silent for a moment and then spoke. "I can tell you this because you've met my father and you've seen how he is." He wiped his mouth with the napkin. "I didn't really want to complete a residency in ortho-pedic surgery, but it was what my father wanted. And it has always been hard living in his shadow, because I never measure up, and he doesn't let me forget it. Did you know he specialized in sports orthopedics? Choosing this fellowship would be exactly what he wants. I don't want to continue living that way."

Dana leaned forward. She understood where Josh was coming from, but there was something he wasn't seeing. "Josh, I hear the nurses talk and whenever a sport-related injury patient comes in, you are the first person they want to call. What does that tell you, Josh? You are good at this and when you add your love for soccer, that's a powerful combination. Can't you see that specializing in this area would be helpful to your soccer clinic dream?

"If nothing else, you would be their first doctor. It doesn't matter if you follow your father's footsteps because now it is also your own dream, and I think it would make you really happy. Just think about it, okay?"

The application for the sports orthopedic fellowship didn't go through the ERAS matching process so Josh could still apply directly to the hospital's orthopedic department. Otherwise, it would have been too late for this year's application process.

"Okay, I'll think about it. Thanks."

The appreciation in his beautiful eyes caused Dana's heart to skip a beat.

"So do you want dessert?" he asked.

"I'll think I'll skip for today. I'm so full! Thanks for such a lovely meal."

"My pleasure." Josh beckoned for the waiter and asked for the bill. The waiter left and then returned two minutes later to inform him that the chef said the meal was on the house. "Tell Marco I said thanks," Josh responded to the waiter. The waiter nodded and left. "We should go," Josh said to Dana.

Dana got up, and Josh helped her with her coat. His touch sent ripples through her body and she reveled in it. He then led her out of the restaurant where the valet was already waiting with Josh's car and helped her into the vehicle before walking over and getting in.

The drive back was quiet but comfortable. They soon arrived at a house nestled in a cul-de-sac in one of the very expensive suburbs very close to downtown Dexington. Dana sat up and turned to Josh. "What are we doing here?"

The electric gate opened, and Josh drove up a short driveway until they stopped in front of a stately grey stone and brick home with large columns. Josh got out and opened the door for Dana. "This is my house. I promised to show you my soap opera collection."

"Your house?" Dana said as she stepped out. "Don't you live with your parents?"

"I stay with them sometimes for my mother's sake, but this is my place, which my grandma gave me before she died." He punched a code into the black box at the entrance and the door slid open. Josh walked into the home and Dana followed behind.

What Dana saw next blew her mind. It was like the house was alive, bursting with colors. There were paintings everywhere, and it was obvious that they were the highlight of the house. The furnishings of the house—from the location of each light fixture to the color of the rugs were decorated to complement them. "Wow! It's beautiful."

"Thank you. It was my grandmother's handiwork."

A painting caught Dana's eye and she walked up to examine it. A mother held a baby in her lap, and the look of pure love as she gazed at her baby, which the painting captured, brought tears behind Dana's eyelids. It reminded her of her mother. "This is beautiful," she said hoarsely. "It's so real."

Dana could smell his spicy aftershave as he stood close behind her. "This was my grandmother's favorite painting."

Dana turned to him. "Your grandmother painted this?"

"Yes, all the paintings you see on the wall. She loved life and tried to show it through all she painted."

"Wow, she was a genius."

"She was the best human being I have ever known," he said with a wistful tone.

"When did she pass away?"

"A year ago. But I still miss her like it was yesterday."

"You must have been close."

"Yes, super close. She was funny, kind, and always told the truth like it is." He chuckled. "Everyone knew not to mess with Grandma. And she always made time for me no matter how busy she was."

"She must have been one special lady."

Josh leaned against the wall. "One time, she took me out as a kid to a restaurant and there was this guy scolding his five-year-old son for peeing in his pants. The kid had been trying to get his father's attention, but the man was busy on his phone until the accident happened. You should have seen my five-foot-two grandma giving this giant of a guy one fierce scolding. She then marched the kid to the bathroom, got our driver to make a run to the nearest store to buy a new pair of shorts and underwear, and she personally changed the kid.

"By the time she was done, the whole restaurant was giving the guy the stink eye. If looks could kill, the man would have died immediately." Josh chuckled. "You should have seen the look on the guy's face. He was so embarrassed and kept wiping his bald head with his handkerchief even though it was cold that day. I think he was afraid of my grandma coming back."

Dana and Josh exploded with laughter. It was just too funny to imagine. Dana leaned against the wall as she held her stomach, which ached from all the laughter. It had been so long since she'd laughed like this. And Josh had been the one to bring it out of her.

She looked at him and he held her gaze. It was like they could see into each other's souls.

This was a different Josh from the one in the hospital, a funnier down-to-earth version that she really liked.

Dana cleared her throat and broke the silence. "What about the soap opera collection?"

Josh smiled at her. "Right this way." He led her beyond the living room to a door down the hallway. When he opened it, Dana gasped.

Rows and rows of either books or DVDs rested on shelves and filled every wall. A large chandelier hung from the ceiling in the center of the room, and plush couches with throws were arranged in various parts of the room. A large oak desk with a matching chair rested on the side of the room facing large windows. It was like a piece of heaven.

Dana stepped into the room and ran her hand along the spines of the books. The faint sweet smell of vanilla flowers and almonds mingled with that of paper and ink and permeated the air. "All these are epic fantasy?"

"Most of them. The rest are other fantasy books that caught my attention," Josh said. 'They are arranged in alphabetical order by author."

"How do you have so many?"

He shrugged and gave her a small smile.

Dana continued to move around the shelves. She saw soap operas from so many different countries, some of which she had never watched. She saw books by her favorite authors, including titles she wished she had but had never been able to get.

"Feel free to pick any two you like," he said. "You can always return them next time."

Dana turned to him and quirked her eyebrow. "Next time?"

By now, Josh was standing close to her. Her whole body lit up from his nearness.

"Yes, next time. Unless you don't want to go out with me again, and I'll respect your wishes."

"I do ... I mean, I don't ... Oh, whatever."

Josh's laughter filled the room. Dana felt her face and ears grow warm. She turned away from him, but a smile tugged at the corners of her lips.

Her phone vibrated and she pulled it out from her clutch. It was her alarm to check up on new patients' notes in the EMR system. She looked at the time and realized it was much later than she had planned to stay.

"Is everything okay?" Josh asked from behind her.

She turned abruptly and almost dropped her phone.

Josh stretched out his hand to steady her. "Take it easy."

"Thank you." She straightened. "It's just time for me to go," she said.

He stared silently at her for a few seconds and moved closer.

Dana's breath quickened. His nearness was making her feel strange things course through her veins. Was he planning to kiss her? If so, she was all for it.

Then he stopped moving as if he'd remembered something, and then stepped back. "Okay, let me take you home," he said.

Dana struggled to hide her disappointment. She'd been sure he was going to kiss her. What had made him stop?

Josh walked over to the desk and pulled out a drawer. He lifted a book with a black hardcover from it, closed the drawer, and walked over to where she stood.

"Here's the latest book from Ted Henderson. You can give it back to me on our next date."

Dana pretended not to hear the comment and gave him a non-committal smile. "Thanks for letting me see your home." But her heart thought otherwise and did some leaping of its own.

Josh smiled at her. "You are the first person I've let in here since my grandmother died."

What did that mean? Was he saying she was special?

"I'll drop you off. Let's go," he said.

CHAPTER 24

The rest of the week flew by quickly with morning reports, newly admitted patients, and surgeries. Josh texted her a couple of times every day, and Dana enjoyed their little conversations.

By the time Thursday rolled around, Dana couldn't wait for the weekend to come. She hadn't been on-call this week, but that could change tomorrow when she started a new trauma rotation. By the time she got home, she was looking forward to dinner with Alicia and Willow to break up the week's intensity.

Dana took a shower and changed into a T-shirt and shorts. Dinner with Alicia was a low-key girls' affair. Jasmine was already back and was catching up on some reading before Alicia arrived.

The doorbell rang. Dana raced down the stairs and opened the door. "Alicia, why did you ring the bell when you have a key?" Dana said, her hands on her hips.

Alicia smiled. "Well, my hands are full. I brought dinner," she said as she lifted the bags in her hands for Dana to see.

"Aunt Dana!" a little voice quipped from behind Alicia and Willow popped into view.

"Willow! I missed you! Come and give me a hug." Dana opened her arms and Willow rushed into them. "How are you doing?"

"I'm fine," Willow said. Her cheeks shone with health.

"And she would be much better if we got her out of the cold and into the house." Alicia stepped past Dana into the apartment.

Dana led Willow in and shut the door behind them. "Alicia, it's not that cold, right, Willow?"

"You know my mom. What can I say?"

"Willow!" Alicia said. Willow and Dana grinned. They liked to tease Alicia whenever they could.

"Hi, Willow!" Jasmine came down the stairs.

"Aunt Jasmine!" Willow rushed forward and gave her a hug. Willow was definitely a hugger.

"How's school been, darling?" Jasmine asked her.

"It's been fun. I have a lot of friends, and I've been invited to sleepovers and birthday parties. And I've been learning a lot from school too," Willow said, her grey eyes bright with excitement. Her beautiful blonde hair had grown into long bangs that framed her face.

"I bet a lot of boys are crushing on you," Jasmine said.

"That's part of school I guess." Jasmine and Dana burst out laughing. Willow never took boys seriously—it had been that way even when she was still staying in the hospital. Good girl. She had her priorities right.

"You guys, I'm starving. Let's eat." Alicia spread out the food packs on the dining table.

"I'll get plates and cutlery," Jasmine said and headed to the kitchen.

The next few minutes were spent catching up on their week as they descended on the food.

"I'm so full," Jasmine said as she leaned back on her chair. "Thanks for the meal, Alicia."

"You're welcome. It's the least I can do." She

turned to Willow. "Willow, why don't you lie down on the couch? You must be tired. We'll leave once I finish chatting with your aunts."

"Yes, Mommy."

Dana smiled just watching them together. This was how it was supposed to be, mother and daughter together, and soon father, once Blake married Alicia. Blake had already completed the adoption process for Willow.

Alicia turned to Dana. "Now, you. What have you been up to? I've been hearing stuff, but I figured I'd wait and hear it from the horse's mouth."

"I've been good," Dana said.

"She has been fake dating Josh," Jasmine said with a chuckle.

"What does that mean?" Alicia looked from Jasmine to Dana.

"Well, I went on a blind date which happened to be at the same hotel where Josh had a blind date of his own, and he ended up telling our dates that I was his girlfriend.

"Then his father heard about it and asked to meet me. And while we were talking with him, Josh ended up telling his dad that we were planning to marry and then it became hard to tell him the truth. So we agreed to keep up the pretend engagement for a few weeks before telling his parents that we've broken up."

Alicia's eyes shone with concern. "Are you okay?" Alicia was the only one who knew her secret. Dana had confided in her after Alicia had pulled her aside about her weird reaction to the truth about Willow.

"I'm fine," Dana reassured her. "There is no mutual commitment, and it's been fun getting to know each other."

"But I think Dana likes Josh," Jasmine interjected.

"Who doesn't like Josh? Alicia, don't you like him?" Dana said.

"I mean she like-likes Josh. And Josh's mother loves her even though his father is well … his father."

Alicia looked at Dana. "Josh is a good guy, and it's okay to like him, even love him, Dana. And from the hints I've gotten from Blake, I think he likes you too."

"But—"

"I know what you are going to say, Dana. But give yourself a chance. You might find out that Josh loves you as you are."

Jasmine looked from Alicia to Dana. "Why do I feel like Alicia is saying one thing but means something else?"

"Aunt Dana?"

"Yes, Willow?"

"I like Uncle Josh, and I want to marry him when I grow up."

Alicia, Jasmine, and Dana burst out laughing. Trust Willow to defuse the atmosphere.

Alicia cleared the table while Jasmine washed the plates and Dana dried them. They soon finished and moved over to the living room where Willow was already fast asleep.

"So how are your wedding plans coming along?" Dana asked Alicia.

"Going great. I'm so thankful Blake's mom hired a wedding planner to help me. I don't know how I would have done it all and taken care of my patients. I feel tired enough as it is."

"We would have helped you if she wasn't there," Jasmine said.

"I know. But we all have busy schedules, so it still wouldn't have been easy to coordinate."

"So anything we can do to help?" Jasmine asked.

"I need you guys to come in for the fitting for the maids-of-honor. I've decided I'll have you both instead of choosing which one of you would take the spot. You can decide how you're going to split up the duties."

"Works for me," Jasmine and Dana said in unison.

"See? I knew you guys would be in sync. So I need you to come in for the fitting both for your dresses and for my wedding dress."

"That will be so much fun!" Dana said.

"Blake is bringing in all the dresses from Italy for the fitting. He would have preferred to fly us all there, but I told him that our schedules for the next few months are crazy. So the wedding planner is going to go with the jet and bring back all the dresses. We'll have the fitting at Blake's parents' home. Any dresses we don't select will be sent back. Blake's mom suggested we make it a slumber party. What do you guys think?"

"That's a wonderful idea," Dana said.

"I'm so down for that," Jasmine said.

"Okay, I'll text you guys the details and the

date and time options once I have a good idea of when everything will be ready. I'm thinking in about two weeks. But we'll adjust based on your actual schedules."

"Sounds good," Dana said.

Alicia leaned back on the chair. "I miss you guys, and I miss this place."

"I wish I could see you more often, but I know you have a crazy schedule," Dana said.

"I can't wait 'til the wedding is over," Alicia said.

"I bet," Jasmine said with a teasing tone. Alicia threw a pillow at her head and she dodged. "What was that for?"

"I'll throw another one if you ask that question again."

"I was just playing with you."

"I can't wait 'til you meet the man of your dreams and it's your turn to receive all the teasing," Alicia said.

A shadow passed over Jasmine's eyes and then disappeared. "That's not going to happen." She pasted a smile on her face. "And right now, we are not talking about me."

Alicia yawned. Dana and Jasmine were quick to follow. They chuckled.

"I think it's time to go home," Alicia said.

"I'll carry Willow to the car for you," Dana said.

"Thanks. Bye, Jasmine."

"Bye," Jasmine responded.

Dana lifted Willow into her arms—she was as light as a feather. She followed Alicia out the door to the red Toyota parked in front of the apartment. It had been a gift from Caroline, Alicia's late sister's friend. Alicia had refused Blake's offer to buy her a car and had asked him to wait until after they got married. Alicia opened the rear door while Dana laid Willow gently into the backseat and buckled her in. She straightened and then closed the door.

"Thanks, Dana," Alicia said. She fixed her eyes on her. "I'm serious about what I said inside. Josh might be the one. And I would be absolutely thrilled if that was the case. Give him a chance and get to know him. You might be surprised to find he is okay with everything." She smiled. "See, you are even blushing, so I know you like him.

"And what if God is the one opening the door? Don't shut it yourself. And when it is right, tell Josh about the situation. If it's God's handiwork, everything will work out. See how He did it for Blake and me. Who would have thought we would be together today? Definitely not me. But it worked out. You are a wonderful lady, so don't sell yourself short."

Dana gave her a hug. "Thanks, Alicia. It means a lot to me."

"Anytime. You deserve love from a wonderful man, Dana. Never forget that." Alicia glanced at the car. "I have to go. I'll see you guys around." She walked over to the driver's side and opened the door. "Bye."

"Bye." Dana watched as Alicia drove away. She climbed back up the front steps. The air had turned a bit nippy, and her legs were freezing. She hurried into the apartment and slid the chain bolt shut.

Jasmine must have turned in for the night— she was no longer downstairs. Dana turned off the lights in the living room and headed upstairs to her bedroom. She entered her room and collapsed on the bed.

Alicia had made some good points tonight. And Dana couldn't pretend any longer. She liked Josh Roman, and not like a friend. Even though she'd given up on marriage, maybe

Alicia was right and this was a God-given chance.

If things didn't work out between them, or if she told him the truth about herself and he changed his mind, she would only be back to square one, which was where she had been all along.

She had nothing to lose and everything to gain.

CHAPTER 25

Starting a new rotation always gave Dana jitters, even one in a department she was familiar with, like the trauma surgery rotation she'd just started. There was a new team of interns and medical students to work with, schedules to figure out, and attendings and other medical staff to bond with. Here, leadership skills were more critical in making split-second decisions for care and coordinating with a wider range of health care professionals.

She had hit the ground running since she'd arrived in the ER at five a.m. and was the day resident on-call until seven p.m. when she would hand over to the night float team. The ER had been busier than usual—so far she had attended to a few gunshot and stab wounds, an inhalation injury, emergency appendectomy, tracheostomy, bowel obstruction, and the dreaded post-cholecystectomy complication case.

The Surgical Intensive Care Unit—SICU—hadn't been better, with numerous calls to see surgical patients with post-operative care needs. It had been great helping patients who needed her emergency care, but she couldn't wait to refill her own tank.

She now had a minute to catch her breath in the call room. Her lower back ached. Dana rubbed it to relieve the strain. Two more hours and she would be done for the day.

Her phone vibrated. She pulled it out from the pocket of her scrubs and looked at the screen. It was an incoming call from an unknown number. Who could be calling her? She answered it. "This is Dana."

"Hi, Dana, it's Tammy O'Brien."

Dana's heart quickened. Did she have news? "Hi, Ms. O'Brien."

Tammy chuckled. "That would be my mother, not me. Just call me Tammy."

"Hi, Tammy."

"Good. I called because I wanted to let you know that I was able to track down my friend, but unfortunately, her children confirmed she had passed away. I just thought you might want to know."

Dana's heart sank, and she reached out with her hand against the wall to steady herself. She'd been so hopeful. "I'm so sorry for your loss," she said.

"Thank you. Her children said she lived a full and happy life. She was that sort of gal. Anyway, I just thought you should know."

"Tammy, thank you so much for everything."

"Sorry, I couldn't really help. Hope everything works out for you."

"Thanks." The call ended.

Dana closed her eyes as she leaned against the wall. Did this mean she would never know about the blood disorder or the name of the surgeon? Why was it so hard to find the information? She wished her day had already ended so she could just curl up in bed.

Her pager buzzed. There was a new patient from a motor vehicle crash. Not again. They reminded her too much of her mother's case.

She let out a tremulous exhale. It was time to put on a strong face for the patient.

She raced to the ER and arrived just as a nurse was setting up the IV line for the patient in his assigned cubicle. She noticed the patient was held down by straps. "What do we have here?" she asked the nurse.

"This is the driver that caused the accident. The family in the other car died and was taken directly to the morgue. He's sustained a deep injury to his thigh that needs suturing to prevent further bleeding."

"Why is he being held down?"

The nurse gave the patient a disgusted look. "He is drunk and has been grabbing and hitting anyone who comes close to him."

Dana tensed and her heart pounded. It was like her mother's death all over again. This monster of a driver had gotten drunk and destroyed an innocent family, just like the driver in her mother's case had done. Maybe there was a little girl just like her who had become an orphan.

Her heart squeezed in pain and she gasped. How could the driver do this? Anyone who got into a vehicle drunk knew that they could possibly kill someone, and yet they did it anyway. Her hands curled into fists. It was murder, pure and simple. She was sorely tempted to just leave him there to bleed away; it wouldn't kill him and would maybe teach him a lesson.

She forced herself to take slow steady breaths. She would not become him. She couldn't forget the Hippocratic Oath she'd taken. And it was not her place to pass judgement on him. The courts would do that soon enough on behalf of the victims. Even if it was killing her, twisting her intestines into coils that were difficult to unwind, she would treat him. She took another deep inhale and exhale.

"Dr. Adams. Dr. Adams."

Dana turned to look at the nurse.

"Do you need anything?" the nurse asked.

Dana relaxed her fists. "Could you get me a surgical pack?" she said in a controlled tone.

"Sure." The nurse walked away and soon returned with a surgical pack. Dana pulled over a chair and sat down. She donned a pair of gloves and examined the patient's thigh. The injury was more superficial than deep, and it appeared no major blood vessels or bones were affected.

She removed the first set of gloves, donned a second pair, opened the surgical pack, and got to work. She cleaned the area with antiseptic, applied a local anesthetic, and forced herself to suture the gash. In a few minutes, she was all done, with the wound dressed.

"You should get the neurosurgeons to come and take a look at him to rule out any cerebral or spinal injuries," she told the nurse.

"I'll page them right away," the nurse said and took the used surgical pack away.

Dana got up. She had done it. She'd known one day she would come face to face with a case similar to what she had experienced, and she was proud of herself for having made it through. But now she was drained, and she needed to lie down even if just for a few minutes.

She left the cubicle and headed toward the call room.

"Dr Adams." Dana turned. It was the same nurse who had brought the surgical pack. "We have another patient that needs your attention. The patient fell down the stairs and sustained both an abdominal injury and a shattered knee. I've already sent a consult to the orthopedic surgeons."

"Where is the patient?"

"This way." The nurse led her to a cubicle on the east end of the ER. Dana swept aside the screen to see a middle-aged man seated next to a woman who was lying on a gurney, an object jutting out from her abdomen. The man was holding her hand and reassuring her. He turned his head at Dana's entrance.

Dana gasped and staggered backwards.

Dana could never forget those eyes. They had haunted her from the day she'd discovered who he was and what he had done. Those eyes had tormented her every time she'd had nightmares about her mother's death, especially when he had been paroled and eventually released. The eyes of the drunken driver that had killed her mom.

Dana couldn't believe it. What was he doing here? He couldn't be related to the woman with the abdominal injury, right?

"Doctor, please help my wife," the man said, reaching out to her.

Dana flinched and took another step back. No, this wasn't happening.

"Dr. Adams—"

Dana didn't hear anything else the nurse said. Her heart pounded in her ears. She had to leave. This was too much. Flashes of memories of her mother's death clouded her vision and she turned and began to walk away.

"Dr. Adams, Dr Adams," the nurse called after her.

Dana ignored her and instead hastened her steps out of the cubicle and down the hallway. Her heart galloped against her ribcage, and she clawed at her chest for air. She needed fresh air, she needed to breathe. And she couldn't fall apart here.

She looked down the hallway and remembered the small conference room at the end of the hallway that was hardly ever used. She could go there.

She rushed to the room and opened the door. It was empty. She raced to the window, opened it, and stuck her head out for fresh air. She gulped deep breaths of air like she was drowning, but her heart wouldn't stop beating fast.

She collapsed on the floor against the wall and dropped her head into her lap. Deep sobs racked her body.

That was when arms encircled her.

Dana looked up with a tear-streaked face.

It was Josh.

CHAPTER 27

Josh had been called to an orthopedic emergency in the ER. He'd been on his way in when he had seen Dana rushing out of the ER and down the hallway.

Josh asked the junior resident who was with him to go ahead and see the patient first. He would join him in a few minutes. The junior resident went ahead, and Josh raced after Dana. She had entered the conference room at the end of the hallway, and he'd followed in after her.

She hadn't even responded when he walked in. Dana sat in a heap on the floor, her head between her knees, wailing like he had never seen before. What had happened?

He quickly locked the conference room and rushed to her side. He knelt down and wrapped her in an embrace.

She lifted her face to look at him, and his heart squeezed in pain at the sight. What had happened? Who had hurt her? He tightened his embrace and rubbed his hand down her back. But it broke a dam within her instead, and she wailed even more.

Josh's nostrils flared. Who had done this to her? He'd never seen her like this. All he wanted to do was make the hurt go away. He was tempted to hunt down whoever had caused this, but it looked like she needed comfort more.

He didn't know how long they stayed that way, but soon her sobs turned to sniffles and then eventually stopped.

Josh stayed silent and continue to hold her in his arms. She fit right in like she belonged there. All he wanted to do was protect her and make sure she was okay.

After a few minutes, she lifted her head to look at him. "Thank you," she said. "I'm sure I look a mess."

"Do you want to talk about it?" he asked quietly.

She stared at him for a moment and then began to speak in a quavering voice. She told him about the patient that had arrived. From the description, it seemed it was the same patient he'd been called to see. She had met the husband of the patient, who turned out to be the drunk driver that had killed her mother in an accident.

Josh felt the air leave his lungs. How had that happened? Of all the hospitals in the area, it had to be the ER where Dana worked and at a time when she was still on duty. He couldn't imagine how she must have felt on seeing him. No wonder she was devastated.

Dana told him what she remembered about the accident that had claimed her mother's life and the ensuing care at the ER. She described how she had gotten the news about her mother's death and what she had later read as the cause of death.

For some strange reason, this somehow felt familiar, but Josh couldn't place where he had seen or read the information. He searched his memory, but nothing came to mind. It was just a coincidence, he concluded. Her mother's death had happened many years ago when he was still a kid, so there was no way he would have seen anything related to her case.

"That's why I don't drive, even though I have a driver's license," Dana said. "It triggers the memory of her death."

She took a deep breath as if unsure if she should go ahead and say it. "The accident stole something else away from me," she said quietly. "Every time I think about it, I remember the driver and I get so angry."

Josh felt a foreboding about what Dana was about to say. Like it was something that had the power to affect him. He swallowed. "What was it?" he asked.

Dana choked back a cry. "My ability to have children," she said.

CHAPTER 28

Josh felt sucker punched, and the air wheezed out of his lungs. How could this be? "Are you sure?" he asked. "I mean, are you certain that you can't have children?"

"Yes," she said in a small voice.

Josh's throat felt dry. He didn't know what to think. How could something so precious be taken away already through no fault of hers? He could see why she was devastated—he would be too if he was in her shoes.

Josh held her closer. Was this why this beautiful woman was still single? She was special, and seeing her like this had made him realize how much she meant to him. She was everything and more than he'd ever wished for in a woman. And she was perfect.

So what if she couldn't have children? They could adopt. Of course, he would have preferred biological children, but adopted children were just as precious. Or they could have no children if that was what she wanted.

Wait! What was he thinking? Marriage and children? His eyes widened. Was he in love with her? He, Josh Roman, who had been running away from a relationship, now wanted to be tied down in marriage? He needed time to process this. But for now, he had to make sure she was okay.

"Hey, look at me." He tilted up her chin so he could see her face. "It's okay, and you are going to be okay." He gave her a warm smile. "And know this, Dana Adams, you are perfect. The fact that you can't have biological children doesn't make you any less perfect. The man who gets to marry you would be the luckiest man in the world, never forget that." He wiped the fresh tears that rolled down her cheeks and hugged her again. "Shh, everything is fine now."

He gave her a few minutes to get a hold of

herself and then got up. He stretched out an arm to her. "Come on."

"Where are we going?" she asked.

"Dr. Adams, I know you may not want to do this, but you have a patient waiting for your help. One that I know you want to save, otherwise you would carry the guilt for a long time."

Dana gave him a small smile, took his hand, and allowed him to help her to her feet. "And how do you know this?"

"Because you are a wonderful doctor who saves lives even when they don't deserve it. And don't worry, I'll be there with you. I also got a consult for the same patient. Let's go."

"I think I need a minute to wash my face. I'm sure I'm a mess."

"You look beautiful to me." Dana blushed. "But if you like, why don't you freshen up in the call room? I'll wait for you until you're done. We can then go together and see the patient."

The smile that lit up her face was worth it.

Josh stood waiting with his hands in front of him as the scrub nurse prepped the patient in the OR. The anesthesiologist sat close to the patient's head and monitored her vitals on the screen beside him. The patient had already been placed under anesthesia, and the surgery would commence in the next few minutes.

The doors of the operating room swished open, and Dana stepped in, suited up in her surgical attire with her hands in front of her. Now he was sure—she looked stunning no matter what she wore. The patient's husband hadn't recognized her, and Dana had decided not to let him know who she was. Josh had agreed with her decision. They had examined and diagnosed the patient and informed their respective attendings of their decision for a joint surgery to address the patient's issues. Their attendings had given the go-ahead for the surgery, so Josh was going to get a chance to operate with Dana at the same time.

This was such a rare opportunity, and Josh didn't know if he would ever have the chance again. He could feel the adrenaline rush through his body as he thought about the upcoming surgery. He'd heard Dana was a really good surgeon, and now he had a front row seat to observe her.

Josh moved over to the left of the patient while Dana moved to the right side. Their respective first assists stood next to them. Then they were fully gloved, and the operation started.

Dana had chosen a jazz piece to play on loop throughout the surgery, which turned out to be one of Josh's favorites as well. And watching her operate was like watching a maestro at work. She moved with grace and elegance, her hands making quick work of removing the foreign object, finding any bleeders and tying them off, repairing any damaged organs, and sterilizing the area before closing the patient up.

The music was like fuel all through the surgery, their movements harmonizing with the ebbs and flows of the piece. This was the first time that Josh had played music during his surgery, and there was no way he could go back to not having it in his OR in the future.

He matched her by performing a knee replacement surgery: he made an incision in the knee area, removed the damaged surfaces of the knee joint, and resurfaced the joint with a prosthesis that attached to the tibial, femoral, and patellar surfaces with surgical cement. Then he closed the incision and attached a drain to remove any fluids. The surgery was completed within two hours. Then the patient was wheeled to the recovery room.

After a brief visit to ensure the patient had woken up and had been sent to the SICU, Dana leaned against the wall in the empty hallway, and Josh did the same. The joint surgery was the last in that OR suite for the day, and the OR would remain closed until the next day when it would be reopened. Only the emergency OR wing would stay open overnight.

"Thank you for your help today," Dana said. "I couldn't have done it without you."

"I'm glad I could help," Josh responded.

They remained in companionable silence for a while and then Dana straightened. "It's time for me to sign off," she said. "What about you?"

"I have to head home. I promised my mother I'd be home for dinner."

"How is she doing?"

"She's fine. She talks about you all the time."

"Please send my regards to her."

Dana turned to face him, and he held her gaze.

Josh's heart rate quickened, and he could

hear himself breathing. The air crackled with electricity. Suddenly, he wanted to kiss her, but he wasn't sure how she would receive it. He didn't want to take advantage of her in anyway.

He saw Dana glance at his lips and move closer. Josh leaned toward her and pulled her close until his forehead touched hers. A spark of electricity sizzled through his body from where they touched.

Josh swallowed. This was it. The pounding in his heart increased as her soft vanilla scent enveloped and drew him close. Her hands reached up and ran through his hair, and he almost lost it. He brushed his fingers against the soft silky skin of her cheek, and he heard her breath hitch and watched her eyes close in anticipation. That was all the invitation he needed.

He pressed his lips against her lightly at first, a soft tender kiss that threatened to undo him as she responded with equal fervor. It was everything he'd dreamed it would be: sweetness, joy, hope, longing, and vulnerability all rolled into one.

It was like a language of its own and he hoped she got the message he communicated from his heart—she was special and perfect just the way she was. He couldn't get enough and deepened the kiss.

When they came up for air, Dana rested her head against his chest, and he held her tight in his arms. No words were needed, and he could have held her that way forever.

Then she reached up and kissed his cheek. "Thank you," she said.

And then she walked away.

CHAPTER 29

Josh entered the house. The lights were still on, which meant his mother had not gone to bed. He had gotten home later than planned. A patient in the ICU had needed his attention. Ten minutes had turned into an hour. He passed through the foyer into the living room and headed for the large winding stairs.

"Ahem." Josh turned to see his father seated at the dining table. His mother was clearing the rest of the placements from the table.

Josh walked over and gave his mother a kiss. "I'm sorry, Mother. There was an emergency surgery and a patient with an unexpected complication that I had to take care of."

"I hope the patients are alright," his mother said with a note of concern.

His father frowned over the black glasses he wore. "You should have called to let your mother know. She spent a lot of time preparing the dishes for you."

Josh's eyebrows rose. His father speaking out for his mother? Had the earth turned on its head?

"I'm sorry, Mother." Josh gave her a hug. She smelled of vanilla, cinnamon, and spice.

"Should I reheat some of the dishes for you?" she asked.

"Thanks, but I'm not hungry. By the way, Dana says hi. The surgery I was in was a joint one with her."

His mother's face lit up at the mention of Dana's name. His father stayed silent, but his face looked grim.

"How is she doing?" his mother asked. "I hope she's not working too hard. I would love to see her again."

Josh winked at his mother. "Soon, Mother, soon. But she just started a new rotation and her schedule is crazy."

"She shouldn't become a stranger."

Josh yawned and grinned.

"Alright, I get it. Off you go. Good night."

"Good night, Mother. Father."

He turned and headed up the stairs.

Josh lay spread-eagled on his bed in a T-shirt and shorts. He'd just taken a hot shower and loved the cool air that was coming through the central air conditioning system. He was as tired as could be, but he couldn't help thinking about what had happened tonight with Dana.

The kiss had been wonderful, ethereal even. He'd had no idea such kisses existed, and he couldn't wait to kiss her again. But more than that, he'd felt her opening up to him like never before and it was a precious gift.

He'd seen a different side of her tonight. She'd been vulnerable, but he'd loved her more for it. It made her seem more human and relatable.

Learning she couldn't have kids had been a shock for sure, but he knew couples who had no issues with their reproductive systems who still were not able to have kids. He knew God had the final say on such matters. And even if it wasn't biologically possible, there were enough kids without parents they could share their love with.

They? Well, it seemed his heart had made up its mind about Dana if he was already thinking along those lines. And the thought of it did not frighten him like he'd expected it to. Some nurses had even mentioned that he smiled more these days, and the only thing different was that Dana was on his mind more often than not.

But was it really possible to have a relationship with her without feeling like he'd been chained? Maybe so, but he wasn't sure. But somehow, he wasn't afraid to try, which was very different from his typical reaction to relationships. And what was Dana thinking? She'd kissed him, but she hadn't said anything. What if she wasn't interested? He had a weird feeling he would be devastated if Dana turned him down.

But was he falling in love? He wasn't sure.

Maybe it was time for a chat with good old Blake.

CHAPTER 30

Dana sat with her back against her bed's headboard and her feet tucked under her legs. She was still shocked about what had happened tonight.

The evening had started off dreary but had ended up on a high. She still couldn't believe that Josh had kissed her. She'd been afraid her heart would collapse from all the racing it had done.

She'd felt catapulted to a different world, one that was bright and hopeful and all happy. From the way he had held her close to the way he'd brushed his fingers against her cheek, only one word had dominated Dana's mind. Precious.

Josh had held her like she was the most precious thing in the world.

When she'd told him about her inability to have children, she had expected him to run as fast as possible away from her. She still wouldn't blame him if he did that tomorrow. It was a hard pill to swallow for anyone, especially when it was obvious that he loved kids. What he was doing with the sports clinic was evidence enough.

But he'd spoken to her like a man who was going to be around for her. But what did that mean really? Dana wasn't sure. She liked the Josh she'd met. He was funny, easy to talk to, passionate about what was important to him, and he understood her and treated her well. And seeing and thinking about him made her heart flutter, though she wasn't sure if that meant she loved him.

And what was Josh thinking after the kiss? Was he planning to just date her, or was he offering something more? If he was considering forever, was Dana willing to open her heart and trust that he would stay wholeheartedly?

She held her head in her hands. Ugh. There

was so much to think about, and yet she needed to go to bed for an early start tomorrow.

A short burst of her ringtone filled the air. Dana checked and it was an email from her mentor, asking her to see him on Monday. Her schedule was usually tight, but she could squeeze out a few minutes of her lunch time. She shot him a quick reply confirming the time and then dropped her phone on the bed.

Her phone pinged. She groaned. What was it this time? She just wanted to shut down all thoughts of Josh and go to bed. She sighed and she looked at the screen. It was Josh. Dana straightened up, her weariness gone, and a smile tugged at the corners of her lips.

Josh: Hope you got home safely.

Dana: I did. Thanks for asking.

Josh: It was great seeing you tonight. I wish we'd had more time to chat.

Dana: Me too.

Josh: By the way, that jazz piece in the OR is also a favorite of mine.

Dana: Really? I absolutely love it. And it always calms me no matter what happens during the surgery.

**Josh: I can see that. Anyway, I'll let you go

so you can get your beauty sleep. Not that you need it, since you are always beautiful.

Dana's face warmed up. Josh definitely had a sweet mouth. Not that she was thinking of the kiss.

Dana: :Smile emoji: Good night, Josh.

Josh: Good night, Dana. Dream of me. :Wink emoji:

Well, she was hoping she didn't, otherwise she would be a mess and not get enough sleep.

CHAPTER 31

The weekend had quickly flown by with a lot of catching up to do for work. So Dana had stayed mostly indoors. She was thankful she had not been on-call this weekend, but it would be the last free one for a while.

Dana had also texted back and forth with Josh. Now she got why some people stayed on the phone all day. Josh was witty, charming, and thoughtful. They'd learned more about each other, and Dana felt like she had known him forever.

Now it was Monday and it was back to work. She'd promised her mentor she would come and see him, and she'd gone to his office once lunch time had rolled around. Dana now sat across from her mentor, a large mahogany desk between them. Prof. Smith was a vascular surgeon—Dana had been matched with him because of her interests in the same subspecialty.

"How are you doing, Dr. Adams?" he asked, his bald head shiny from whatever oil he had used that morning. Prof. Smith was known for being conscientious about grooming his head, not that Dana had seen any hair on it since she'd known him. But he more than made up for it with the smooth blonde hair that graced his forearms, visible from rolled-up sleeves.

"I'm good. I just started a new rotation, trauma surgery, and I'm getting back into the swing of things," Dana responded.

"Good. I'm sure you are probably wondering why I called you in to speak with you." Dana nodded. "I had a chat with your attending from your last rotation, Dr. Kelly, and she only had great things to say about you and commented on how you are such a natural with children. She used the word 'genius.' Have you considered doing a fellowship in pediatric surgery instead?"

Woah. This was not what she'd expected to hear today. The idea had crossed her mind before, but she'd always shoved it away because of her situation. She'd decided it would be too much torture to take care of children when she couldn't have kids of her own.

"It's not something I've spent time thinking about," Dana said truthfully. "And I do like vascular surgery, and the hours are not bad either," she said with a smile.

"True. But are you passionate about it?" Prof. Smith said as he leaned back. "This profession is already grueling enough as it is, and what makes you stick with it day and night is your love and passion for the work. Then it becomes a thing of pleasure and not a chore. Dr. Kelly and even the Chair of the Pediatric Surgery Division, Professor Tan, are more than willing to serve as your co-mentors if you decide to go that route. Why don't you think about it and let me know later what you decide? And take your time. There is no hurry."

Even the Chair of Pediatric Surgery? He wasn't known for endorsing people easily. Maybe there was something they had seen about her that she wasn't aware of. "I'll think about it and let you know what I decide."

"Good. I won't keep you. I'm sure you haven't had lunch. I'll talk to you soon."

Dana got up. "Thanks, Professor." She let herself out of his office.

She took the elevator to the lobby and walked over to the café in the east wing of the ground floor. Dana selected a wrapped ham sandwich and a bottle of water and paid for it at the checkout counter. But her mind kept ruminating on what Prof. Smith had told her.

Pediatric surgery. She had enjoyed it more than she'd thought possible even though she had tried to hold herself back so she wouldn't get hurt. But selecting it as a fellowship would mean spending the rest of her life working on it —a lot longer than the one-month rotation she'd done. She wasn't sure how she felt about that. She needed to talk it over with someone who understood.

She left the café and walked over to a quiet corner near the bank of ATMs at the northern wing of the floor. She pulled out her phone and sent Josh a quick text.

Dana: Hey, are you busy?

Her phone rang almost immediately. She

pressed the answer button. "Hi, Josh." She could hear voices in the background.

"What's going on? Are you okay?" Josh said from the other end of the line.

Why was it that his voice never failed to make warm butterflies pop in her belly? "I'm good. I just wanted to run an idea by you. Is this a good time?" Dana asked.

"Give me one second."

Dana noticed she could no longer hear the voices.

"Okay, I've found a quiet place. What's up?"

"Well, I just had a discussion with my mentor and he wants me to consider a fellowship in pediatric surgery instead of vascular surgery like I've always wanted."

"Were there any special reasons why he brought it up?"

"My former attending, Dr. Kelly and Professor Tan would like me to consider it."

"Professor Tan? That's high praise coming from him. But how do you feel about it?"

"I don't know. I mean I like it, but I've always pushed it out of my mind because well … I can't have children and I figured it would be torture. Now I don't know."

"Has that thought changed?"

"You know, when he raised it, I wasn't as closed off to it as I've been in the past. I think just talking about it with you helped."

"But which do you like better: pediatric surgery or vascular surgery? Which do you think would keep you up at night thinking about ways to become better at it?"

"I'm not sure. But I feel like pediatric surgery might do that a bit more. When my mother was alive, she used to comment how much I enjoyed helping out other little kids."

"Here's what I would suggest: assume you are starting with a blank slate and have not selected any fellowship. Why don't you spend time learning more about both fellowships? Talk to fellows and attendings in both areas about their experiences in these services. Read articles on them and learn as much as you can. And talk to your peers and former classmates who are looking to work in either area to see what they think the pros and cons are. Then gauge which one you are more drawn to and interested in. And it never hurts to pray about it."

"I would never have pegged you as a religious fellow," Dana teased him.

"I'm not, but I would be a fool not to recognize we have a God who is probably much wiser than us. That's what I believe. To every man his own."

"Okay, I'll do all the above. Thanks again for taking the time to hear me out."

"Always my pleasure, Dana. You are that special to me."

The words warmed Dana's heart and her face creased into a smile. "You don't hold back, do you, Pretend Fiancé?"

"Well, I could certainly do more than talk, if you want," he said in a low voice.

Dana remembered the kiss, and her ears grew warm. "Bye, Josh." She heard his laughter as she quickly ended the call.

"Hey, what are you so happy about?" Dana looked up to see Lilly walking toward her.

"What are you doing here?" Dana asked.

"I came to withdraw some cash. But I can see you are up to something. Do you have a boyfriend? A date? Give me all the details."

Dana smiled. "Lilly, I have to go. Duty calls, and I still need to eat."

"Wait!"

Dana waved at her over her head and headed to the ER.

There was no way she was going to tell her about Josh and how he had become special to her.

CHAPTER 32

"That wasn't so bad now, was it?" Blake said as he sat across from Josh in the coffee shop. They had just finished their tux fitting and had decided to grab a cup of coffee before heading back to the hospital.

"Good thing you insisted on using our tailor. Traveling to Italy for a tux fitting was not in my schedule for this weekend," Josh said.

"Monsieur Trenton is just as good if not better than some of those designers. His exclusive clientele list is probably more robust. And he already knows what works for our bodies. I'm glad I talked my mother down on that one."

"So how is the rest of the planning going?"

"Thankfully, I don't have a lot on my plate.

Alicia and I have gone through the guest list with my parents. She wants a medium-sized wedding instead of a large one, and I'm trying to give her that without stepping on my parents' toes. So far, it's working well, and I haven't heard any complaints from either my mom or her."

"What about the transition work? How is that going?"

"It's going okay. I have a good team."

"Is Alex Cunningham still giving you issues on the hospital board?"

"Not at the moment, but I'm staying cautious. He's the kind of guy you have to stay watchful against. Wasn't it his daughter that was on the blind date with you?"

"Yes, it was, and I'm so glad I dodged that bullet."

"So I assume things are working out between you and Dana? Alicia wants to know what you are up to. She is worried that Dana will get hurt and will kill me if it happens. I don't know why she wouldn't kill you instead."

Josh grinned. "You know I'm special to her."

"Yeah, right. But seriously, what's your plan?"

"Tell Alicia to back down. I've got this. I know we started off with a fake relationship, but now all I can think about is her."

"I can't believe this. Josh Roman has fallen in love. That's like the miracle of the century." Blake grinned. "I remember a certain somebody who didn't want to be shackled to anyone else."

"I know, right? But the thought of being shackled to Dana actually sounds intriguing."

Blake chuckled. "Are you still my friend Josh? I never thought I would hear 'shackled' and 'intriguing' in the same sentence from you."

"Anyway, I really like her and want to ask her to be my real girlfriend. Baby steps for me, you know."

"But?"

"I have to tell her about Grandma's inheritance, which isn't, in itself, such a big deal, since Dana isn't the materialistic kind. But I worry she will think I planned the whole fake engagement thing just to inherit the money, which wasn't really how it happened."

"A relationship needs to be founded on truth. And trust me you don't want her to hear about it from someone else." Josh remembered how Blake's relationship with Alicia became rocky when he didn't disclose his friendship with Laura, a childhood friend who had been his late brother's sweetheart and not his.

"Okay, I'll tell her. Better now than later. I'm just going to go for it."

"That's my boy. You can do this."

Josh checked the time. "I think we should get going. I still need to check on a patient in the SICU before I head home."

He felt eyes on his back, and he turned around but didn't see anyone he recognized in the café. There was a blonde lady whose face he couldn't see, but she was wearing a blue beanie and black glasses. Not a combination he'd seen with any of his friends or acquaintances.

"What is it?" Blake asked.

"It's nothing." He picked up his phone and slipped it into his jacket. "Let's go."

CHAPTER 33

Dana dropped her work bag on the desk in her room. She was the only one at home—Jasmine was working on her research and had said she would be back late. Dana had been lucky to leave the hospital on time, but her luck was likely going to run out one of these days. She was exhausted, and a nice soak in the bathtub would be great.

She'd spent last night and today taking Josh's advice about the fellowship options to heart. She had reached out to her classmates who were pursuing similar fellowship options, and a few had even offered to connect her with fellows who were already in the program. What she'd learned so far had been enlightening. Still, it wasn't enough for her to make the decision one way or the other—she had her own personal research left to do. There was still enough time to figure it all out.

A smile creased her face. She had received a call from Josh last night asking her out on a date tonight. She still had some time before he was due to arrive. She'd already picked the outfit—a simple long sleeve floral dress that she'd always received wonderful compliments on but never really had the chance to wear as much as she would have liked.

About an hour later, she was ready. Her phone vibrated. She picked it up and checked the screen. It was a text message from Josh, informing her that her ride had arrived and was waiting outside. The doorbell rang at that moment.

Dana picked up her clutch, stuffed her phone and wallet in it, donned her jacket, and rushed downstairs. She opened the door to see a smartly dressed middle-aged man wearing silver-rimmed glasses standing on her front steps. What looked like a Rolls-Royce Phantom limousine lounged by the curb. "Can I help you?" she asked.

"Good evening, ma'am," the man said. "This is for you." The man extended a phone to her.

Dana took the phone and held it against her ear. "Hello?"

"Dana, it's me, Josh." It was him alright, because he was the only one whose voice had the power to make her skin tingle.

"Josh, what's going on? Where are you?"

"That's your ride. He'll bring you to where I am. I just wanted you to know that I sent him. See you soon."

"Alright." She handed back the phone to the chauffeur.

"This way, please." The chauffeur opened the rear door of the limousine for her to enter.

Dana stepped in and settled into the plush custom-stitched leather seating. Her eyes swept through the interior, and she smiled. It boasted —in addition to other features—dual LCD flat screen TVs that were displaying a recent episode of a soap opera that she'd missed watching, an invisible audio system that was playing a soft jazz piece, a hardwood center console icebox with chilled bottles of water and sparkling apple cider, and fade-to-off interior LED lighting. Josh had outdone himself to provide an environment that appealed to her.

She settled into the seat and closed her eyes. Any remaining tiredness she'd felt had faded. This was one of the things she loved about him —his sensitivity and care. He understood her, and when she conversed with him, he stayed fully focused on her, like she was all that mattered. And her heart sang whenever she saw him, heard his voice, or received a text from him. Did this mean she was falling in love with him?

Her phone vibrated. She opened her clutch and looked at the screen. It was a text message from an unknown number. Not many people had her personal number, so this was strange. She unlocked her phone and read the message:

Josh Roman is only interested in you because he needs you to inherit his grandmother's wealth by the end of the month. From a concerned citizen.

Dana's phone clattered to the floor near her feet, and she bent down to pick it up. Her heart pounded loudly in her chest. There was no way it was true. Josh would have told her if that was the case. Maybe not in the beginning, but he would have told her by now, given how close they had become. There was no way he was keeping something as important as this from her.

Dana's hands shook as she stuffed her phone back into her clutch. Did it mean everything had been fake? Had Josh pretended to like her only to get what he wanted? No, the Josh she knew wouldn't have done that. There had to be an explanation. And this text message could just be a lie. Josh was well-liked, and maybe it was someone who was jealous and didn't want them to work out.

She took deep breaths and let them out. There was no need to jump to a conclusion because of one text. She was seeing Josh tonight, and she would ask him. He would tell her the truth. She was sure this was all a mistake. Yes, there was no sense in getting ahead of herself.

The limousine came to a stop. Dana ran a hand through her hair and smoothed out her dress and coat. The passenger door opened. "This way, ma'am," the chauffeur said and reached out a hand to her.

Dana took his hand and stepped out to the sidewalk. She looked up at the building in front of her and gasped. Jazz 213! It was a famous jazz club in Dexington that only opened on Fridays and hosted the top jazz ensembles from all over the country.

She'd heard the owner was very rich and wasn't in it for the money; all he wanted was to provide the ultimate experience for true jazz fans. She'd tried a couple of times to get a ticket to any of its events, but she'd never been successful—it was always sold out. What were they doing here? Thoughts of the text message tried to fill her mind, but Dana brushed them away. She could wait to hear from Josh.

A doorman greeted her and opened the door to the club. Dana stepped in to the sounds of the opening bars of an oldie jazz piece she loved. The interior was larger than she'd expected, and the center had been cleared of the tables and chairs that filled other areas of the room.

And then lights came on centerstage and Dana gasped. The jazz piece was being played by the original band! Her hand flew over her mouth. And they were looking at and singing to her! Dana didn't know whether to fangirl or maintain her composure.

And then a man walked in from the side and

began to sing the lyrics of the song. At this point, Dana was afraid she would pass out. It was Josh! His rich baritone voice hit the highs and lows of the song perfectly. And the words wrapped around Dana's heart and warmed her. When he sang "You are the only one I want in my life," tears rose unbidden behind Dana's eyelids and threatened to escape down her cheeks.

But thoughts from the text message crashed through her mind. Was this all real, or was it smoke and mirrors? Did Josh mean what she thought he was saying through the music, or was he just trying to coddle her until he got what he wanted? Dana shook her head. These thoughts were taking away from what could have been a special experience for her, but she couldn't stop them.

The piece came to an end, and Dana plastered a smile on her face and clapped for the group. They took a bow and then left the stage. Now, only Josh remained and he dropped the mic and walked toward her. He stopped close to her, and Dana fought the urge to step back. She couldn't wait any longer. She had to find out.

"Dana—"

"Josh, did you stick with the fake engagement just so you could inherit your grandmother's estate?"

Josh's face blanched, and Dana's heart squeezed in pain and she staggered back. He didn't have to utter a word—the expression on his face said it all. So it was true. She'd refused to believe it and had hung onto the hope that it was all a trick. She had to get away.

She turned and fled from the club as tears poured down her face.

"Dana, wait! Let me explain!" she heard him say from behind her, but she didn't turn back.

Right now, she just needed to get as far away from him as possible.

Dana rushed past Jasmine and raced up the stairs.

"Dana, what's wrong?" Jasmine asked with concern.

Dana entered her bedroom, flung herself on the bed, and covered her head with her pillow.

She heard Jasmine enter the room, and the bed dipped when she sat down beside her.

"Dana, what's wrong?" Jasmine asked tenderly.

"I just want to be alone," she whispered.

"Okay. I'm here anytime you want to talk." Dana heard her get up and then leave the room, shutting the door quietly behind her.

And then the tears came. It was like a tap she couldn't turn off. This was what she'd been afraid of—opening her heart to a man who wouldn't marry her and who had instead torn her heart to pieces. She had been right; she wasn't made for love. And Dana cried at the thought of a life without love and for the future her that would always miss him.

CHAPTER 34

Dana rubbed her forehead as she typed her notes into the computer terminal at the ER's central nursing station. She'd developed a splitting headache on waking up this morning and taking some painkillers hadn't helped.

She'd cried for a long time last night before finally falling asleep. She'd switched off her phone when it kept ringing from Josh trying to reach her and had seen a lot of missed calls, voicemails, and text messages from him when she switched it back on this morning. Dana had ignored them all. Jasmine had made a hot breakfast for her and left it on the dining table. Dana had nibbled on a tiny bit before giving up.

She'd forced herself to come to work this morning. Her patients needed her, and it would be a good distraction from the turmoil her heart was in, because Josh had wormed his way into her life and her heart still longed for him despite the betrayal.

But there was no way she was going to let him back in. As painful as it felt, she had to get over it and move on no matter how long it took. She'd also brought his book along and had left it with his junior resident to return to him.

She felt eyes on her, and she looked up. The nurses who had been chatting with each other went silent. What was that all about? She focused back on finishing the notes. She had another patient waiting for her. Once she was done, she signed off, and then headed up the elevators to the SICU. The patient, Ms. Hernandez, had been admitted overnight with a ruptured appendix and had received an appendectomy. Dana needed to make sure there were no complications.

She saw the nurses at the central station give her furtive glances as she passed them. First in the ER and now the SICU. This was getting weird. She touched her face but felt nothing. So why was she getting all these looks?

"Dana."

She turned to see her colleague, Lilly, beckoning to her out of one of the cubicles. Dana strode to where she was.

"Hey, Lilly. What's up?"

Lilly pulled her into the empty cubicle and looked around before turning to her. "Dana, have you heard the rumor? They are saying that Josh roped you into a fake engagement, and the only reason was to get his grandmother's money. Is it true? What's going on?"

Dana felt the blood drain from her face. So this was why everyone had been behaving strangely around her this morning. She had been afraid of this from the beginning, and it had finally happened.

How had the news gotten into the hospital's rumor mill? It couldn't be Josh. There was no way he would embarrass himself this way. Then it was someone else. Who could it be?

Then she remembered last night's text message from the so-called concerned citizen. Whoever the person was had known the truth and had most likely spread it. But despite the person's malicious intent, the sad fact was that it was all true. How was she going to survive in the hospital now? And Josh's father. Dana prayed he hadn't heard the news.

"Dana, are you okay? Is it true?" Lilly's voice jolted her back to the present.

Dana gave her a small smile. "I'm okay. Look, I need to go see my patient. I'll talk to you later." She left Lilly standing there and headed straight to her patient's cubicle. She checked Ms. Hernandez and wrote some additional orders and then left the SICU.

She took a deep inhale and exhale as she waited for the elevator to arrive. She had done nothing wrong and would face this issue head on. All she had to do was focus on her work and ignore everything else, which was easier said than done.

Switching off her phone would be a good start.

CHAPTER 35

"What's going on, Josh? I thought you said you were going to take care of Dana," Blake said from the other end of the line.

Josh ran his hand through his hair as he paced the call room. He'd just received the book from his junior resident, but had not been able to catch a glimpse of Dana herself. Thankfully, the junior resident had left immediately, and the call room was empty. Maybe the other residents had gotten a memo to stay clear of him. But he was grateful for the solitude, whatever the reason for it was.

He couldn't believe what was going on. Only yesterday, Dana had found out about his grandmother's inheritance, and now the whole hospital knew. If only he had gotten the chance to tell her the truth yesterday as he'd planned. Now she must think the worst of him: that he had spread the rumor. "Blake, I planned to tell her last night, but somehow she found out before I could."

"Alicia is mad at me now. You need to fix this."

"I called and sent Dana text messages but she's not answering. I called again a few minutes ago and it went to voicemail. She's most likely in the ER, but I'm afraid I'll just be adding more fuel to the rumor if I go to look for her there. I really don't know what to do."

"What about your father? Does he know?"

"I'm not sure. He hasn't called me, but that doesn't mean anything."

"Let's assume he doesn't know yet. Is there anything you can do to turn this around? We can't allow this to hurt Dana more than it has already."

Josh racked his brain. How could he fix this? How could he convince Dana that his feelings for her were real? How could he let her know that he loved her?

Because that was what had happened. Josh Roman had fallen in love with Dana Adams. He had realized that when she left yesterday. He'd felt so empty, and only knowing he had patients and a medical team depending on him had made him come to work despite everything. He just wanted her back in his life.

An idea popped into his mind. This could work. "Blake, I have an idea. I need to go."

"Okay. Good luck, buddy. I'll wait for the good news."

"Thanks." Josh ended the call. He had no time to lose. He quickly changed into his street clothes, picked up his car key fob, and left the room.

CHAPTER 36

Dana sat cross-legged on the couch and stared at the TV. The painful day had finally ended, and she was glad to be back home. The whispers at work had continued throughout the day, but she'd tried to ignore them as much as possible. Even some of the patients had caught onto what had happened and had given her pitying stares.

She couldn't continue crying and needed a distraction. Soap operas were out of the question because they reminded her too much of him, and she'd settled for flipping through the channels.

A news flash caught her attention. A crumpled black car was visible on the screen, and it reminded her of Josh. Dana leaned forward to hear what the reporter was saying, and her hand flew to her mouth.

No, it couldn't be. There was no way he'd been in an accident. But then they flashed a picture of him at the top corner of the screen, saying the accident had happened a few minutes away from the local courthouse. He had been transported to the Dexington Medical Center for treatment.

Dana jumped up from the couch. Her heart beat fiercely against her rib cage, and she wrapped her arms around herself to stop the shaking.

She had to go to him. Even though things were over between them, her heart already belonged to him. She had to make sure he was okay.

She raced upstairs, grabbed her spring jacket, wallet, and keys, and rushed outside. While she waited to see if there were any cabs she could hail, she called the cab services in the area. But they all had an hour delay, and there was no way Dana could wait that long.

She ran to her bike that was chained to the decorative iron work that fenced their front yard. She rarely used it during winter and spring, but it would work for today. Then she looked down and saw that one of the wheel spokes had broken. Dana sighed. She'd planned to replace the wheel but had then forgotten about it. What was she going to do now?

That was when she remembered Jasmine's grey Mercedes. Jasmine had given Dana permission to drive it whenever she wanted. A part of her recoiled at the thought. She'd avoided driving over the years after what had happened to her mother. What if she had an accident?

No, she couldn't be thinking about this. Josh needed her and she had to hurry. She could do this. Dana rushed back into the house and grabbed Jasmine's car keys from their spot in one of the kitchen cabinets before running back out. The car was parked by the curb in front of the house and Dana unlocked it and slipped in. The interior was still warm, which meant that Jasmine had used it earlier today. She checked the fuel gauge—the tank was full. Good.

Her hands shook as she gripped the steering wheel, and her stomach coiled with tension. She took a long inhale and exhale and pressed the ignition button. The car roared to life, and Dana carefully checked the street before swinging out of the spot onto the road.

Her heart was in her mouth the whole time she was driving, and when Dana reached the hospital entrance, she was just glad she had arrived safely, even though she had slowed down a couple of times along the way.

She didn't remember giving the valet the car keys, but the ticket in her hand was evidence that she had done so. She ran into the ER; at this point she didn't care what anyone thought about her behavior. Her eyes darted around the area as she tried to figure out where he could be.

"Dr. Adams, are you looking for Josh?" Dana turned to see Stan Temple had reached her side. She'd seen him working with Josh before, and the camaraderie that she had witnessed between them indicated they were more than acquaintances. He would know where Josh was.

Dana nodded, her heart still maintaining its frantic pace.

"He's already been taken to the VIP floor," he said.

Dana muttered a thank you and hurried out of the ER and down the hallway. She rode the elevators to the VIP floor. There was a large concierge station near the entrance, and Dana walked up to it.

She'd never had the privilege of being on this floor; the fellows and attendings were the ones who dealt with such patients. "I'm here to see Josh Roman," she said as she flashed her hospital badge at the ruddy-cheeked nurse that had stepped up to attend to her.

The nurse took her hospital badge and typed on the computer in front of her. Then she looked up at Dana and handed her badge back. "I'm sorry, your name is not on the list of visitors to see Dr. Roman."

Dana's heart increased its pace. She had to see him, to make sure that he was okay. "Is there no way I can see him even for a little while?"

The nurse gave her a set smile. "I'm sorry. Only approved visitors can see a patient on this floor."

"You can let her in," a voice said. Dana turned to see Blake coming from the direction of one of the rooms. "She is his fiancée. Please add her to the family list and include that I authorized the visit."

Dana hurried over to where Blake stood.

"How is he? Is he okay?" Her voice choked with the last words.

"He is going to be fine. I'm sure he'll be glad to see you. Go on." He motioned in the direction of the last room on the right.

Dana sped down the hallway and stopped in front of the door. She took a deep breath and then opened the door gently and stepped in.

Josh lay on the hospital bed with his eyes closed, his left foot in a cast and an IV line snaking from his left arm to the IV pole next to his bed. The rhythmic swoosh and beep from the monitor was the only interruption of the silence that filled the air.

Dana choked back a cry and rushed to his side.

"He is only sleeping." Dana hadn't heard the nurse come in.

Dana watched as she changed the IV fluid and hung up another bag. Then the nurse reached down to the lower section of her mobile cart and pulled out a designer satchel Dana had seen Josh use occasionally and a black hard-bound book. "A detective just stopped by to drop these off. They were found in Dr. Roman's car." The nurse extended them to Dana.

Dana accepted the items and then looked around for where to place them. By this time the nurse had wheeled the cart out of the room. There was a large closet, and Dana headed toward it. As she opened one of its doors, the book slipped and fell on the floor, and a document fluttered out.

Dana picked it up, opened it, and stilled. She couldn't believe what she was seeing. It was a notarized document stating that Josh was giving up his rights to his grandmother's inheritance. From the value written on the document, Josh was giving up more than a billion dollars' worth of estate.

Her knees became weak, and she shoved the items into the closet and made it back to the chair beside his bed. There could only be one reason Josh would do that—to prove to her that he loved her for her and not for what he was hoping to gain. Such a huge amount of money would have helped him realize his long-term dream of building soccer clinics nationwide. Yet, he had given it all up for her.

She didn't deserve him. But he'd helped her realize she could still be loved as she was. She tried to hold back her tears, but a few still slid down her cheeks. Josh stirred, and Dana straightened. She'd seen that Josh was okay. That was all she'd needed to know. It was time to go.

She turned to leave, and a hand grasped her wrist. She looked back to see Josh's eyes had opened. "Please don't go," he said in a tired voice. Dana's eyes searched his. She could see the gold flecks in his eyes and the remorse registered in them. "Please," he repeated.

He tried to sit up, and pain flashed in his eyes. "I'll help you," she said as she reached to support him from falling back. She adjusted the pillows behind him and made sure he was comfortable. Then she sat down on the side of the bed.

"Dana, I'm so sorry about what happened," Josh said. "I should have told you about the inheritance. I had planned to tell you that night, but you found out before I could."

"I got a text message about it from an anonymous person."

"I'm assuming it was the same person that spread the rumors in the hospital."

"That's my guess as well. I'm sorry I took off without hearing you out."

"Dana," he reached out a hand to touch her cheek.

His touch sent zaps and tingles through her skin. She leaned into it. She had missed this.

"When I thought I had lost you forever, that's when I realized how much you meant to me," Josh said. "I didn't just want you as my girlfriend, I wanted you in my life forever. I wanted you to know I loved you even without the inheritance, and the only way I knew to prove it was to give it all up.

"I was on my way to the courthouse to file the paperwork when the accident happened. A child ran into the road, and I had to swerve to avoid him and ended up hitting a pole. I'm just grateful I'm alive to see you again. Dana Adams, would you forgive me and make me the happiest man alive? Would you marry me?"

Dana stared into his eyes. All she could see was the love he had for her, and her eyes watered. She loved this man who had stolen her heart and who loved her as she was. "No," she said.

His face mirrored the confusion he probably felt. "Why?"

"I'll consider it only on one condition."

"What is it? I'll make it happen."

"You promise?"

"On Scout's honor."

Dana lifted an eyebrow. "I didn't know you used to be a Boy Scout."

"No, I wasn't. Dana, stop teasing me! I'm a patient, remember?" Josh wriggled his eyebrows.

Dana laughed. "Okay, okay, I'll tell you. On the condition that you tear up that document in the book. You and I will probably make more than we need in a lifetime. But your grandmother probably left it to you to help you achieve your dream. You need it for the sports clinics. You could create a foundation for it if you like."

"Okay, I'll tear it up. And that is a fantastic idea about the foundation. So, will you marry me?"

Dana beamed at him. "Yes, Josh, I'll marry you."

He leaned forward as if to kiss her and then stiffened. "Ouch, it hurts." He gave her a sheepish grin. "I forgot I had a broken rib."

"Don't worry. You'll have more than enough chances in the future," Dana said and winked at him. She watched Josh's face grow red. Who would have thought? Now she'd found something to tease him about. "And in good news, I drove myself to the hospital today."

Josh's face lit up in wonder. "You did? Congratulations! That's cause for celebration." His hand caressed her face. "I love you, Dana Adams," he said and kissed her fingers.

"I love you, Josh Roman." Dana got up, leaned forward, and gave him a sound kiss on the lips that sent all the butterflies in the world to her insides.

CHAPTER 37

Dana swallowed as she got out of the chauffeured car. Josh had ended up with a sprain on his foot, but Dana had insisted he not drive for a week to help it heal, and Josh had acquiesced.

Josh had also called in a custom jeweler, who had designed the perfect engagement ring that was easy for her to wear as a surgeon. Alicia, Blake, and Jasmine had been happy to hear the good news about the proposal. Willow had accepted it good-naturedly. And the news had made its rounds in the hospital once her colleagues and nurses saw the engagement ring.

Josh's father had finally heard the first rumors and had demanded an explanation.

Dana and Josh were supposed to have dinner at Josh's parents' house tonight—they would break the good news to them then.

Dana had felt her mouth grow dry as Josh ushered her into their home. Now they were seated in the living room, his parents on one couch, and Josh and Dana on the other. Dana bit her lip, but Josh covered her hand with his. He gave her a reassuring smile and Dana's shoulders relaxed.

"So, is it true? Was your engagement fake?" Josh's father asked.

Ouch. Straight to the jugular.

"Yes and no," Josh said.

Josh's father frowned. "What does that even mean? You are either fake engaged or you are not."

"It started off as a fake engagement, but I really proposed to Dana, asking her to marry me and she said yes."

His mother sprang up and gave Dana a hug. "See, I knew she was the one."

"But that's not the point," Josh's father said. "You lied to us."

"I'm sorry about that," Josh said. "But Dana didn't lie. The first time she heard about it was when I mentioned it to you in your study, and she was too stunned to say anything. She had nothing to do with it."

Dana patted Josh's hand. "It's okay, Josh. I was wrong for even going along with it." She turned to Josh's parents. "You didn't deserve that. I should have told you the truth."

His father stayed silent and then said, "I don't think she is the one for you. So it's a no from me regarding this marriage."

Dana felt a heavy feeling settle in her stomach. There was no way the wedding could happen until they got his father's approval. Josh might want to barrel ahead with it, but Prof. Victor Roman was important to Josh even if he wouldn't admit it. And the last thing Dana wanted was to create a rift between father and son.

His mother turned to his father. "Why? I think they are perfect together."

"I said no. I'm against this marriage," his father said.

Dana's phone vibrated at that moment. She pulled it and discreetly checked the screen. It was Tammy O'Brien. Her pulse quickened. She'd thought she wouldn't call her again. Or had she found out something? It was also a good excuse as any to step away from the tense atmosphere. And some things were better said when only family was around.

She sprang up and let go of Josh's hand. "Please excuse me for one moment. I need to take this call." Dana didn't wait for a reply and stepped into the foyer. They probably wouldn't miss her with the ongoing argument. She answered the call.

"Hello, Tammy," she said.

"Hi, Dana." Dana could hear a lot of noise and music in the background. "I'm at a reunion and I met a nurse who had worked with my friend in the ER. She remembered the name of the doctor my friend had a crush on at the time."

Dana's heart pounded. "Who was it?"

"Dr. Victor Roman," Tammy responded.

A sudden coldness hit Dana at her core, and she staggered and leaned against the wall. Now it all made sense.

"Dana? Are you still there?"

"Thank you, Tammy. This is very helpful."

"Alright, I have to go," Tammy said above the background noise. "Let me know if you ever need anything else. Good luck with everything."

"Thanks, Tammy." The line went dead.

Dana shivered, and she wrapped her arms around herself. She took a minute to process what she'd heard. Then she straightened and walked back into the living room. Josh and his parents sat in cold silence.

Dana sat down beside Josh. Her body still shook. "Hey, Dana, what's wrong?" Josh asked with a concerned look.

Dana faced his father. "Is this why you don't want me to marry Josh?" she said quietly. "Is this why you had that strange look on your face the first day I met you in the study?"

A look of panic crossed his father's face. "What do you mean?"

"Because I'm Dana Adams, daughter to Sienna Adams?"

His father's face paled. So it was true.

Dana's heart tightened in pain, and she almost doubled over.

Josh looked in confusion from his father to Dana. "Dana, what are you talking about?"

"Remember when I told you that my mother died on the operating table? I just got a call that a Dr. Victor Roman had been the surgeon at the time."

Josh's eyes widened, and he looked at his father. "Is it true, Father?" His father stayed silent.

"Did she die from a rare blood disease?" his mother asked in a disbelieving voice. How did she know?

"Yes, that's what the death certificate said," Dana responded.

"Oh my goodness! It's that case," his mother whispered.

Josh looked from his mother to his father. His father slumped defeated into the couch. "What's going on? What case?"

His mother turned a dazed look at Josh. "The case that changed your father."

CHAPTER 38

Dana listened as Josh's mother recounted what she knew about the case. "Your father was a young doctor at the time and was still building his career. Dana's mother was the first person to die on his operating table, and he was devastated. Even after a thorough investigation was done and he was exonerated, he carried the guilt around like a heavy load.

"Many nights he couldn't sleep and I would find him head down in his study looking through documents and searching for an answer. At the time, much wasn't known about your mother's blood disorder, so it wasn't a routine test and she hadn't been diagnosed with it at the time.

"But your father blamed himself, and from that day on, he swore he would never have another table death and would be the best at what he did. He measured himself against a high standard, the effects of which unfortunately spilled over into our marriage and his relationship with you."

"So, that's why he was very strict with me. Many times I wondered if he even cared about me. He always seemed disappointed in everything I did."

"I'm sorry I didn't intervene as much as I should have. Many times I thought about leaving your father. Sometimes he was like a stranger and not the man I married, but then I would remember how he used to be before everything had happened."

"So that's why Dana's mom's case seemed familiar when she told me about it. I used to sneak up to Father's study when I was younger and read some of his old surgical notes."

"But that still doesn't explain why Professor Roman doesn't want me to marry Josh," Dana said to Josh's mom.

Josh's father sighed. "Because I know my son, and I know he'll carry the guilt around for the rest of his life if he marries you. And it would affect your marriage like it did mine. It's enough that I've suffered. I don't want my son to go through the same thing I did.

"I have nothing against you, Dana. I have actually liked you from the first day I met you during the orientation and have watched your progress in the residency program. And then I heard someone had been digging into the case, and I found out it was you, Sienna Adams' daughter."

Dana's heart broke as she watched him. He looked dejected and sad. Her mother's death had not only affected her but Josh's family as well. Josh's father ran his hands through his hair and then looked at Dana with unshed tears. "I'm so sorry about your mother," he said in a strangled voice.

At his words, Dana broke down and cried. Josh's arms encircled her and soon his mother's joined his as well. She wept for the death of her mother, for the life she had lost, and for the wreckage it had caused in Josh's family. Once her tears were spent, she looked up at Josh's father.

"Professor Roman, I need to know. Was my mother's blood disorder hereditary?"

"No, it wasn't," he was quick to reassure her. "She had paroxysmal nocturnal hemoglobinuria, which you probably know has an unknown cause and is not hereditary."

Dana felt like a heavy boulder had been rolled off her shoulders. She'd had this mystery hanging over her head for most of her life, and it was a relief to finally know the truth. She now had peace in her heart, and she wished Josh's father would have the same.

She got up and walked over to where he sat and then gave him a hug. "I know it wasn't your fault, and I forgive you. I hope you'll forgive yourself. I know my mother would want the same." She felt him tremble and she stepped away. He needed this time alone. And Josh's mother got up and went over to sit with him.

Josh appeared by her side. "I think we need to give my parents some space," he said.

Dana nodded and followed Josh to the foyer, where they donned their jackets. Josh faced

Dana and gave her a hug. "I love you so much, Dana Adams."

"And I love you, Josh Roman," Dana responded.

She had finally come home.

*D*ana waited at the door to Josh's parents' home.

"I'm coming!" Josh said as he wrangled a wriggling four-year old with curly hair in his arms. He opened the door and Marcel jumped down from his arms and rushed into the house.

"Grandpa," Marcel screamed.

Dana smiled at Josh as they followed him in. It never got old.

"There you are, my little munchkin." Josh's father came into view as he scooped Marcel into his arms.

"Grandpa, I played soccer."

"You did? I'm so proud of you."

Marcel beamed. Dana watched them with joy in her heart. After she and Josh had gotten married, they had travelled to Spain for their honeymoon and to visit Josh's soccer team. There, they had fallen in love with Marcel, an orphan who had been abandoned in front of the club's soccer clinic, and had adopted him. And it was the best decision they had ever made. Marcel had brought so much joy into their lives and was Prof. Roman's favorite person.

"Hello, Dad," Josh greeted.

His father smiled in return and gave Dana a hug. "You look great," he said.

Dana's face warmed. She would never get tired of the transformed Prof. Roman. He'd become like the father she'd never had.

Josh looked around. "What about Mom?" Josh asked.

"She's determined to make the perfect lunch and made a quick trip to the grocery store to grab a last-minute item. She should be back soon," Josh's father said. "Linda also called and said she was on her way with Mike."

Josh led Dana to a couch. "Here. Let me help you." He guided Dana until she sat down. She tried to adjust, but it was hard to do so with two footballs in her womb. The doctors said it was a miracle.

Dana was now a pediatric surgeon, while Josh had become a highly-sought-after sports surgeon. The soccer clinics were now in twenty-one states, and the demand for them in other states was growing. Their lives were always busy, but family remained their number one priority.

Dana felt a tightening in her belly, and her face scrunched up. This was not the first time today she'd felt it, but it was now coming with some regularity.

"What is it, honey?" Josh asked with concern written all over his face.

"It's time. I think Elena and Sienna are on their way."

Dana took a deep breath and then relaxed.

She had her own Billionaire Owner Doc.

Everything would be alright.

Thank you so much for reading! Want to know

what happens next in Dexington, and how Jasmine, Dana's best friend, finds love (an arranged marriage romance)?

Check out LOVING THE BILLIONAIRE ARMY DOC at https://dobidaniels.com.

Here's an excerpt:

David froze. "What?" This must be some kind of joke. They couldn't be serious about this.

"I know it sounds strange in this day and age to talk about an arranged marriage," his mom chimed in. "But when I found out who their daughter was, I figured it was worth a shot."

His mother must be kidding. It didn't matter who the girl was. There was no way he was getting married, especially to someone he barely knew. But his curiosity was piqued. Who was this girl that could make his mom, the great advocate for all things love, change her mind? "And who is this young lady?"

His mom gave his dad a look before responding. "Jasmine Banks," she said.

David stiffened. It had been a long time since he'd heard that name, but all the memories associated with it came flooding back. His chest tightened like a boulder had landed on it. He forced himself to take a deep breath. "Jasmine Banks? The same one from high school?"

"Yes," she said.

David couldn't help but laugh. His parents had finally lost their marbles.

There was no way he would marry Jasmine Banks, not even if they tied him up and dragged him to the altar.

Want to read more? You can grab LOVING THE BILLIONAIRE ARMY DOC at
https://dobidaniels.com!

Or want to know what happens next in Dexington?
Sign up now at https://dobidaniels.com.

If you've loved reading Loving the Billionaire Owner Doc, Dobi would be grateful if you could spend a few minutes to leave a review (as short as you like) on the book's page on your favorite retailer. Your review would help bring it to the attention of other readers. Thank you very much.

Check out all Dobi Daniels books at https://dobidaniels.com

ACKNOWLEDGMENTS

Writing a book is harder and more rewarding than I could have ever imagined. And it would not have been possible without the support, love, and encouragement from my number one cheerleader, my dearest mom. My life would never have been this awesome and wonderful without you.

Of course, I have to thank my precious little DC for his smiles and antics. You brighten my day and give me the strength to keep pushing through.

Thank you to my sisters for encouraging me on this wonderful journey. And a special thanks to my baby brother (who is so not a baby anymore) for being super supportive and checking in on my progress. You guys are the best.

Thank you to my wonderful author friends. You know who you are. Your selflessness and willingness to share what you know has made my writing journey smoother and an exciting one. And a special thanks to Lisa and Deanna whose support have made a difference.

Most of all, I want to thank God who gave me life, surrounded me with the most wonderful people, and loved me all the way. You make my life complete.

And finally, a special thanks to all my readers whose love of my stories spur me on to write more. Thank you!

ABOUT DOBI DANIELS

As a former physician and business executive in another life—with a childhood filled with reading multi-genre novels—Dobi Daniels loves to write sweet thrilling romance stories with heart. She enjoys dreaming up everyday characters who rise above unfavorable circumstances to overcome incredible odds and find joy along the way.

When not writing, Dobi can be found binging K-dramas and ice cream with her little sidekick by her side.

Loving the Billionaire Owner Doc is the second book in the Dexington Doctor Billionaires Series. Sign up at dobidaniels.com to be notified when the next Dobi Daniels book comes out!

Thank you!

https://dobidaniels.com
hello@dobidaniels.com
facebook.com/dobidaniels
bookbub.com/profile/dobi-daniels
instagram.com/dobidaniels